I0685278

WINTER AWAKENING

Dana Bell

Wolfsinger Publications   Security, Colorado

ISBN 978-1-936099-07-8

Printed and bound in the United States of America

ACKNOWLEDGEMENTS & DEDICATION

Contrary to popular mythology, writers don't secret themselves away, write a book, and it magically appears in publication. There are hours of research, sometimes travel, and the other people who read and suggest changes to the original manuscript, not to mention other unexpected influences. This page is for all those who helped make *Winter Awakening* a reality.

First off to God, for giving me the talent and imagination. Thank you. I could never have written this book without Your guidance.

Second to my resident felines Maximillian and Sammy who have blessed my life in so many ways and appear in these pages as characters. Also to Little One, Tabitha and Dids who have now passed beyond and wait for me in heaven.

Third, to my husband for his love, support, and encouragement.

Fourth, to Andre Norton and her use of animals in her books. Christie Golden for her willingness to answer my questions during OPUS about the publishing world. Denise Little, Hillari Bell, Carol Hightshoe, Sarah Hoyt, David Boop, and others, who have heard me read from this manuscript at conferences or conventions and for their helpful feedback.

Fifth, a special thanks to Carol Meyer who read and edited these pages despite having to search for her lost dog in the Garden of the Gods. I'm sorry you never found him, but am happy you chose another to bless your life.

Sixth, to the Colorado Wolf and Wildlife Center for the VIP tours they give and the chance to meet a wolf muzzle to face. You're doing a great job educating the public about these wonderful creatures. Also the naturalists at Yellowstone National Park, and several other centers dedicated to wolves. I also want to thank the Denver Zoo, Cheyenne Mountain Zoo, and San Diego Zoo for the chance to observe wolves and Snow Ghosts.

Seventh, to Dr. Richard Fleck for the ice aged themed writing assignment that inspired the original short story, *To Rule Again*, which I completed in Art & Craft of Writing. Also, to Dr. Theresa Crater and the Science Fiction Workshop class of 2002. All of you helped in the birthing process and the feedback given was invaluable.

Eighth, to anyone else I may have forgotten to include. You know who you are. My thanks to all.

Prelude

B. I blinked my eyes in surprise. B. The first human letter to unravel itself to me. B. I tried to read the next letter in the word. I cocked my huge, brown furred head. The next letter reminded me of my turquoise eyes or the round grey tunnel I had used, on my last distance hunt, to escape a gang of wild butt sniffers. O. O is the next letter! I concentrated on the last. Images of tree branches forking in two directions sprang into my mind. I squinted in the fading daylight as my eyes adjusted to the change. Y…Y…Y.

I sat on my haunches. I glanced from the picture on the page and tried to correlate the image to the three letters. B…O…Y. An old story floated into my memory. Miah, the Elder of my mother's den, had told me a tale once, well, more times than that actually, about the humans who had once inhabited this vast frozen waste.

"The planet was infested by them," he had croaked. "Ugly, hairless creatures with no respect for us, butt sniffers, scurriers, or any living creature." He scratched his ear. A sure sign he was annoyed. "They didn't even respect each other. Always stealing, killing, digging up the land with huge metal monsters and covering it with sprawling solid rocks.

Their offspring, the girls and boys, weren't any better."

B.O.Y. Boy. A small male human. Child. Kitten.

Kitten! A human male kitten!

Excited, I twitched my bushy tail. Now, I needed to figure out the next word.

Chapter 1

It had been at least twenty-four full moons since I had last seen my mother. I paused before entering her lair. Scented all around the entrance was the urine of a male I didn't know. The need for caution rose in me. I slipped past the floppy flap, the old rickety door squeaking like a caught scurrier.

My mother spotted me at once. She hissed, arching her long tan back, her short fur raised in spiked defiance.

"Hello, Mother," I greeted warily.

"Half Breed," she snarled.

I knew she'd never forgiven my father for lowering her status from Purebred to Mongrel by mating with her. She'd never liked me either, her half Abyssinian, half Maine Coon son. (I'd learned the humans had once called us that.) As a result she'd taken out her hatred of my father on me. While she'd raised my half siblings with tender love, she'd only given me basic care. When I was old enough, she'd thrown me out.

"Half Breed," she spat again, making it sound like a coughed up hairball.

I'd always hated my name. With her contempt of me, I've always been thankful to Bast that I looked more like my father than her. I'd seen my reflection in old broken mirrors. My fur was long, brown with irregular black stripes and a solid body with large paws equipping me well for cold and snow.

"And why have you wandered back here?" My mother's yellow eyes glared at me.

I pretended to be disinterested by cleaning a spot on my shoulder, noticing she was heavy with a new batch of kittens.

"You should be out there fighting for Mongrel females and breeding!" Her thin tail flicked from side to side. "Not that any would have you!"

I wouldn't bother to tell her I'd only been in a few challenges—none of which I'd won. My defeat would only confirm her low regard of me. Sitting down, I curled my tail over my paws, pretending a calm I didn't feel. "I've been doing more important things. Like learning to read."

"Nonsense!" she sneered. "What use is human knowledge! We know all we need to know. Hunt. Mate. Survive."

"Do you not wish for more?" I quietly asked her. What part of me had secretly wanted her to be proud of my accomplishment?

"All I had your father took from me!" she screeched. "My mates now are only Mongrels! No Purebred will ever have me again!"

"And she has a new mate." A large black male joined us from the dim shadows. I hadn't noticed him before. Perhaps he'd entered through a way I knew nothing about.

Instinctively, I rose, puffing my fur to look bigger, watching for the potential weaknesses and strengths of the other.

His gold eyes raked over me. He stopped beside my mother and gave her a friendly lick. She cringed.

"I'm Midnight," he introduced himself stepping in front of his female.

"Half Breed."

His fur formed a hard ridge down his narrow back. "You're not welcome here."

I glanced at my mother while keeping alert for any aggressive movement from her new mate. Her eyes sent hate filled claws into my soul. She'd never accept me nor the challenge I could issue to add her to my den. So be it.

I moved slowly toward the exit. "Good bye, Mother. I won't return."

"Good." She crawled away to her ratty nest.

Her mate followed me out, watching as I hopped through the snow. I stopped several body lengths away, checking to make certain he wasn't following. His black body darted back behind the flap. Evidently, he didn't think me a threat.

A breeze twirled over my fur. I lifted my black nose and sniffed the dampness of storm scent. Heavy white clouds rested on the far mountains and I knew they'd soon drop their burden. I needed to find shelter before the snow fell.

Brushing the icy coldness with my belly, I darted through the thick crusted snow, pondering what to do next. I knew I had wandered much, never making a permanent den, taking temporary shelter in abandoned buildings or hollow trees. Yet, I would need somewhere to raise my kittens and teach them, and it needed to be defendable.

Hopefully, any future females I won would be agreeable to my plan.

I had no intention of being like the other males. Impregnating females, leaving them to raise the kittens alone, expanding my territory, always wandering, always fighting.

But, where to establish my den? I caught a whiff of a high hunter, wolf, I corrected myself, and changed my path to avoid meeting one of the cunning canines.

Visions of the school where I'd learned to read caused me to stop and consider. The brick building was very large and had many good places to hide. Scurriers were plentiful so we'd never go hungry. Old coats, books, and other odd things littered the paint peeling hallways. Yes, this place of human learning *would* be the best. It would good for my future kittens to learn in the same place where I had begun my education.

I bounced off, leaping joyfully through the drifts. My huge paws, part of my father's heritage, helped me easily cross the plain. My thick fur protected me from the bitter cold.

A faint squeak reached my ears. I slunk down, intensely listening. Deep in my throat I start the hunting chant.

Hide.
Listen.
Watch.

Grey blur.
Soft squeak.
Prey.

Slink.
Track movement.
Wiggle butt.
Pounce.

Catch.
Toss in air.
Play.

Tear hide.
Warm.
Eat.

Thank, The Provider.
Leave a blood offering
For Bast.

~ * ~

"The female's name is Tomura. She is, by all I've heard, a beautiful Purebred Shiya". All Purebreds were known by their original sire's name. Humans called them Siamese. "Her bronze fur glistens with fastidious cleanliness. Her paws, ears and tail are deep brown. Her eyes are almond shaped and chocolate colored." Wistfully, Mikki, an older grey mix described Tomura. She'd soon to be in heat. "Not that we'll get to challenge for her, we Mongrels. No doubt, Chien, this season's champion, will win her."

I had decided to attend the local male gathering. We always talked of potential females and upcoming challenges."I hear she's proud and talks down to males," Talhal commented, shaking his rusty shorthaired head.

Intently I paid attention while pretending not to by washing my ear. I'd heard Siamese produced large litters and usually always succeeded in raising them to adulthood. Not a common thing with Mongrel batches.

"She does," Mikki acknowledged. His wise eyes drifted over all of us. We all understood here we were friends, but at other times we must be rivals.

"She also speaks fanciful tales of us once being worshipped. Seems to think we should rise to our proper place once again." Talhal blinked, our form of laughter.

Others blinked too. Secretly, I decided she might be a good mate for me.

"Tomura speaks about planning for a feline future," Mikki continued. "Being only concerned about hunting, mating and raising kittens is not enough for her."

Talhal sneezed. "Chien can have her. I want a female who knows what is important."

"As do I," Mikki agreed. "She is a rare beauty though."

"A beauty but too haughty." Talhal rubbed against Mikki. The two were long time friends. "What other females are coming into heat?"

The two went on about others while many unmated males listened. I stayed through the gathering, but heard nothing of others with the type of promise Tomura held. I hoped she'd agree to allow me to issue a challenge.

As morning neared, we paired off in play fight practice. I needed to sharpen my battle skills if I wished to win a female as far thinking as a certain Shiya Purebred.

~ * ~

It took me five full sunrises to reach Tomura's den. I hesitated on the worn wooden steps. My mother had hated my father for daring to lower her status. Would Tomura treat me with the same contempt?

I muttered a quick prayer to Bast. Vague reassurance seemed to reach me and I dared to enter the partially open door of an old "Victorian" house. At least, that is how the humans had described them, though their famed 'Grand Lady' status was long gone and faded. Chipped and cracked paint adorned the graying dwelling.

Looking around, I heard a challenge in progress. Trotting quickly over faded rugs, I found the room where two Siamese males tumbled. Recognizing the white mass as this season's champion Chien, I hopped up on the back of a tattered chair to watch.

His opponent howled and retreated from the battle, a deep and long gash bleeding down his side. He murmured the traditional, "I yield."

Chien stood victorious, his sides heaving.

"You seem to have another challenger," a silky female voice mocked.

Chien turned blazing blue eyes on me. "Mongrel!" he spat, spittle tinted red dripping to the floor. "You have no place among we Shiya!"

"I have the right of challenge, if Tomura agrees." I tried to sound confident. My heart beat rapidly. By right, she could refuse and I would leave without my intended prize.

She materialized out of the gloom. Her chocolate eyes studied me. "And you are?"

"Half Breed."

She eyes widened slightly in surprise as she looked up at me. She sat gracefully, her thin brown tipped tail tucked daintily over her paws. Certain she would refuse my challenge I jumped down, preparing to leave Chien with his rightly won female.

"You may challenge," she finally deigned.

"What!" Chien bellowed. He glared at her, "You arrogant," he suddenly sprang at me.

I ducked to the side and whirled around striking with my claws. The Shiya hissed, trying to return a blow. Lunging for his neck, I sank my teeth into soft flesh. He attempted to shake me loose then went limp, falling to his side. I sensed his back claws tense and knew he was going to try and rake my vulnerable underside.

"Yield, Chien," Tomura ordered.

"No!"

"Yield. Half Breed has bested you." She rose and approached us. "I wouldn't have you now."

At her hard yet rightful words, he breathed, "I yield." His eyes though, spoke his full fury. I waited a heartbeat before releasing him. I stepped back and tensed for a possible second attack.

He slowly got to his feet, snarled at me, then her, and sulked off, his belly brushing the floor in defeat.

Fighting the urges of my body, for I wanted desperately to mate with her, I asked, "Why did you agree to the challenge?" I had expected her to react as my mother had.

She rolled onto her back rubbing her body on the dusty floor. "I've heard of you, Word Warrior. It is said, you are the first of us to read the human language." She rose and touched my nose with her soft tan one. "I think you will be great amongst us. Why would I not want to bear your kittens?"

"I'm a Mongrel. Mating with me will lower your status."

"What do I care of status if my kittens can learn to read?" She licked my face. Her wise almond eyes beckoned me. "Claim your rightfully won prize, Word Warrior." She crouched down.

Word Warrior. I liked the name. Maybe I would claim it as my own.

~ * ~

Our litter arrived many sunrises and hunts later. I fathered four males and three females. Tomura birthed them during a gloomy, snowy sunrise. Gazing into her carefully constructed nest, I watched their small wiggling white bodies. My mate had just finished cleaning the last one to have been born. It struggled beside its siblings and grabbed one of her tits.

"We'll know their true colorings in several moonrises," she tiredly told me. "My mother told me they'd be white at first." Tomura closed her eyes and laid back to sleep.

I conceded to her wisdom. Females knew more of these matters than males. Certain she and our kittens were warm and comfortable, I settled on an old coat I had found. I'd dragged it into the classroom where we had made our den. Closing my eyes I napped, listening for any potential danger.

When I opened my eyes, Tomura was bathing one of our kittens. She noticed me. "The sun is now shining. There is no hint of more snow. Perhaps you should hunt, Word Warrior."

Languidly I stretched, feeling the muscles of my back relax. "Do you need a break?"

She finished cleaning the kitten and picked up the next one. "No. Later perhaps."

Padding across the chilly floor, I jumped up on the windowsill to look outside. Pristine ivory glistened. Some skeleton trees reached into the sky. Nothing moved. I jumped down. I would go down the hall to the cafeteria. That was where humans had once prepared their food.

The rats lived there. I wasn't always sure what they found to eat, but at least my mate and I had a steady food supply. Clinging to the shadows, I managed to catch one quickly. I broke its neck and dragged it down the long hall and offered it to my mate. She sniffed and made motions to bury it.

Hurt by her rejection of my gift, I wondered if she expected me to go outside and see if I could find a rabbit or perhaps a rare bird.

"Aren't you hungry?" I asked.

"No." Carefully she rose, trying not to disturb her now dozing brood. "I need a break now."

I crawled in next to our kittens. Snuggling down to keep them warm, I enjoyed the feel of their small bodies. I almost wished they were awake so I could hear their tiny purrs. Tomura soon returned and we changed places. When they awoke she nursed them, bathed them again, and encouraged them to sleep.

Choosing to nap as well, I circled my tattered coat, and settled in, kneading the wool. I pulled myself into a tight ball and settled my tail over my nose.

"Do you ever tire of this cold?" Tomura inquired.

"Yes."

"I've heard stories it was once different."

"The books I've read say it once was. There were warm seasons."

"I wonder if it will ever change." Tomura started to purr and her lilting voice filled the room.

Soft purr
quiet song,
suck well my baby.

Grow fast,
live long,
sire your own young.

Sleep well
young one,
grow up to hunt.
I will
teach you
how to eat rat.

Feel my
strong tongue
cleaning your body.
I will
care for
you until you're weaned.

Soft purr
quiet song,
sleep will my baby.

I closed my eyes contentedly. I listened to her continued purr, meant to relax and reassure our kittens, and allowed her motherly skill to lull me to sleep.

~ * ~

Heavy snow draped the landscape in denseness obscuring my sight. I pulled my dead flapper through the growing drift. Fortunately, I had found and killed a rarely found goose. Tomura had tired of rat and her complaining about our rodent diet had finally driven me outside despite the dreadful weather.

I paused as my ears picked up the eerie howl. Though the wolf packs rarely journeyed here, I had been scenting their urine more often. Perhaps their hunting had become poor and they now intruded into our territory. I'd have to ask the other males about it at our next gathering. For now, I would need to be watchful and elude their hunters.

Hopefully, the falling snow would mask my scent and make it more difficult to be tracked. Besides, I didn't want to lose my hard-earned goose.

My mate would voice her strong objections and more than likely insist I go out to hunt again if I failed to provide her with a 'worthy' meal.

Listening intently since my life depended on it, I slowly crawled up a slight incline, dragging my flapper. I sank down into the cold drift and peered below. A shaggy two leg grunted, and just barely, I heard the fear filled mew of a kitten.

Chapter 2

I watched the two leg as it lay on its belly, one of its dirty appendages extended into a cat-sized tunnel. A burst of wind brought the stench of unburied waste. I gagged. The creature didn't seem to know it needed to bathe. It was easy to scent.

The kitten mewling increased to higher desperate octaves. I growled deep in my throat. Since my own brood had arrived, my protective instincts had grown stronger. That disgusting creature threatened one of my own kind and I had the overwhelming urge to help despite having to fight my strong instincts to leave the youngster, who was not mine, to its fate. Besides, unless my ears deceived me, it didn't sound much older than my own.

Wondering why a female would turn out such a young kitten, I watched for a heartbeat longer. An angry feeling filled me as I saw the slain body of a female lying in a pool of spreading red. I just caught her sweet sticky scent of death.

My anger grew. I ignored the thick flakes pelting my fur and the slow drizzling wet trickling to my skin. For one of us to die in a challenge, to starve, to lose to the butt sniffers, these fates where acceptable. But be prey for a two leg!

Slowly I backed partially down the incline. Digging a shallow hole, I buried my goose. It should be safe there for a short while.

Bouncing back up and skidding down into the small gully, I daringly pounced on the two leg. Hopefully, this one hunted alone like us and not in a gang like the sniffers. It looked blankly at me. I released a piercing battle scream and waited for its response.

The two leg pulled its appendage out of the tunnel. The sharp edges left dripping red scratches on it splattering the snow.

I hissed, moving backward, daring it to follow me. The creature grabbed at its middle, and almost too late, I realized it could trap me. I caught its throwing motion and the whirling shape in the air. I dodged to the side and the net fell into the snow a body length away.

I yowled a challenge running toward a grove of pine trees. The two leg ran to retrieve its net and tried to run after me. The deep snow hindered it and it floundered like a rightful kill dying.

At the edge of the woods, I looked back to make certain it followed. Out of the grove a wolf dashed circling around behind the two leg. My hunter stopped apparently confused. The wolf darted in and nipped the creature. The two leg squealed rat like.

Not sure how to handle a sudden unexpected ally, I dashed into the trees, using the low branches to hide. I heard the two leg flounder into the pines. I glanced back and saw the wolf leisurely lope after it.

Somewhere close there was a place we could lure the two leg to its death. I knew of a deep hole from many past hunting trips. I dashed out into the open wanting the two leg to see me again. It did. It struggled after me, vainly trying to toss its net, which tangled in the branches.

I flew over the hole, barely covered with loose wood, and hid under a thick snow covered branch. I heard a crunch and a horrified bellow as it fell to its death. I poked my head out. The wolf stood at the edge, looked down at the two leg then at me. The high hunter yipped once and ran off.

Odd. I had always thought they considered us prey.

After a couple of heartbeats I caught my breath. When I finally considered it safe, I looped around the trees, keeping a watchful vigilance. I had no desire to encounter another two leg, or even a wolf, no matter how odd the behavior.

The wind blew, forcing its freezing claws into my nose. I bent my head against it, fighting each step back to my buried goose. Reclaiming my prey, I skidded back down into the gully, pausing to breathe a prayer to Bast to receive the soul of the slain female and backed into the grey tunnel forcing my kill through the hole.

I knew, from previous excursions, the tunnel system tended to interconnect. With snow falling heavily I would be safer following them back to my den.

Now, where was the kitten?

I waited, trying to ignore the roaring wind echoing through the tunnel. Faintly, I heard the kitten crying. Trying to follow the deceptive sound, I made a few wrong turns, before finally locating the small youngster hunched in a tight cold corner.

Stopping a body length away I struggled with my male instincts. They instructed me to kill this kitten who was not my own. However, I had read many accounts telling of humans who had once raised other males' young as their own.

The kitten sneezed.

I knew I needed to get this kitten to Tomura and have my mate warm the youngster before it froze to death. I owed the kitten's dead mother that much. She'd obviously died protecting her young.

Dropping my goose, I spoke softly. "I won't harm you." The kitten didn't reply. It just sat shivering. Tentatively, I stepped forward, taking it gently by the neck suppressing my urge to kill it. Setting it down on the grimy ground, I dried it with my tongue, purring to reassure it.

"I'm cold," the kitten whispered.

"I know." I pushed it to its feet with my nose. "Can you walk a little ways? I'll take you with me."

Woeful green eyes looked up. "I think…maybe…I can."

I grabbed my goose by its floppy neck and set off in the right direction. Glancing back, I saw the kitten shakily following.

Dirt and mold fell from the roof into my fur. I would definitely need a good wash once I got back. I pressed homeward, wanting to clean up and get warm on my woolen coat.

We emerged just under the rusted out grate of the school's cafeteria. I leaped out clumsily pulling my prey up and onto the floor, checking quickly for any rats, who might be tempted to try and steal our meal. I saw none and reached down and caught the kitten by the neck again putting it down beside me.

"This way." I grabbed the goose and trotted down the hallway to the classroom we denned in. The tiny kitten glanced around curiously, but scurried to keep up with me.

Tomura jumped down from the windowsill as we entered. She ran to me and licked my face in greeting. She shook her head and spat out grim. "You need to wash yourself."

I dropped my kill before her. "Your feast."

She sniffed the goose. My mate glanced at me and the kitten, who had plopped on the cold floor and was shivering violently.

"I rescued it from a two leg. It had slain the mother."

Tomura nodded her understanding. "Poor thing." She gathered the kitten into her mouth and took it into her nest. She cleaned the tiny youngster. "A female," she informed me, before urging the kitten to nurse. "You need some warm milk. Drink."

The female drank some and shyly snuggled close to Tomura. My mate reassuringly nuzzled the youngster and purred. She finally fell asleep.

I proceeded to defeather my prey and offered a choice bit to my mate. She nibbled the meat and soon finished the feast. I ate my share as well.

"Why?" Tomura asked me. "Beyond the two leg killing her mother. Males never take in the kitten of another."

Uncertain I tried to explain. Lamely I said, "I couldn't leave her to freeze."

Tomura's silence informed me she was considering my words. "Wash," she ordered. "You smell of stale water and mold."

I slowly started to clean myself. After the wonderful meat, the grim from the tunnel tasted rank. "How old is the kitten?" I asked as I paused my cleaning with my tongue.

"About two full moons."

I'd been right. She was just a little older than my own.

"In another eight, she'll come into her first heat."

"And?"

"She could be a potential mate."

"Perhaps."

"Word Warrior, you need more females,"

"I've heard rumors of one called Starlite. She will come into heat during the half moon."

"The one with the 'sight'?"

"Yes."

"Well, then. You should challenge for and win her."

Chapter 3

Polana stared across the vast frozen water, her eyes traveling to the shrouded peaks of what must surely be the domain of the snow ghosts. Her parched mouth begged for a drink as she skirted the edge, searching both for a crack and a possible place to build her nest. Soon, her heavy stomach reminded her. One of her kittens stirred poking a tiny paw against her side. She paused until it quieted before continuing on.

Something bright and slightly jagged jutted out of a deep drift. Before the sky could drop more of the miserable white stuff on her, she hurried toward it, stopping on what seemed a stable patch. It shifted under her paws and she slid downward into a place that blocked her from the constant wind. Gazing back the way she'd come, she saw two giant structures kept partly open by high drifts.

Slipping inside she touched a chilly floor. She lifted one paw and cautiously advanced, sniffing the air for possible predators. Her eyes grew accustomed to the dim light and though the smell of old death lingered, nothing else had denned here. In one place she found bones, shreds of warm cloth she could use for her nest, and other objects broken and scattered around.

Her search led her to a small place, large enough to build her nest, and hidden enough her kittens would be safe while she hunted. She worked until the moon rose gathering what she needed to make a warm and secure place. Tired from her journey she settled down and slept, rousing only as the constant and annoying wind rattled the structure. Since the cold didn't penetrate where she was, she ignored it and returned to her slumber.

As the sun approached, so did the pains announcing the pending arrival of her kittens. The next moonrise three lay dead. She'd properly dispose of their remains as soon as she finished cleaning her one surviving male. He was all white and she was curious what color his eyes would be. He wouldn't open them for many moonrises. His tiny body wriggled until he found her tit and grabbed it hungrily. At least she'd have plenty of milk for him.

Once he'd finished she washed him again and placed him in a cozy corner. She cleaned the nest and disposed of the bodies of her dead young. Tasks completed she curled up next to her kitten to keep him warm. She tried to ignore the howling wind filled with a mourning whine similar to a lonely high hunter she'd heard often.

Thoughts of the hunters caused her to lift her head. Her ears twitched listening for any sound signaling a predator and danger to them both. Hearing nothing but wind, she closed her eyes. Her body cried out for rest after not sleeping for so very long. Unable to resist, she gave in.

~ * ~

She tried not to stay away long by hunting and eating the small squeakers who infested the structure. Soon though she tired of the little meat they provided. Polana began to take longer excursions outside to hunt and not just to relieve herself.

A long storm settled in dropping more and more of the wet white. She shivered in the biting cold as the wind raked her fur with sharp cruel claws. With a tug she dragged the short tailed grounder toward her nest. She'd spent half the sunrise hunting the elusive creature and now felt she deserved the feast of her kill.

The sharp scent of a hunter caused her to drop her meal. Sides heaving she stood still, glancing quickly around trying to spot the potential predator. Nothing moved so she took her meal inside and dropped it near her kitten. He wobbled over and sniffed. His eyes had opened a few moonrises ago and she was surprised they were a clear blue.

Polana hadn't decided on a name yet. She watched in amusement as he batted at her kill. Vague memories of her mother doing the same with her floated through her mind and she was certain this was how to teach him about potential prey.

He bounced around her prey for a few heartbeats and crawled back into the nest. Poking her head in to check on him, she saw he'd curled into a tight ball and fallen asleep.

Attacking her kill as if it were still alive she ripped out flesh, savoring the tangy taste of blood and meat. She ate as much as she could unsure of when her next meal would be. She washed her fur meticulously and curled into the nest with her kitten.

She'd earned her nap.

Howling awoke her. Her ears twitched and her heart beat wildly. If they found her she might be able to escape but she knew they'd kill her kitten. After losing the other three she had no intention of allowing him to die. Bast could not be that cruel!

Slowly she crept out of the nest quietly placing her paws on the cold floor. Brushing her belly against it she used anything she found to try and hide her presence. When she reached the entrance blinding white blocked her view.

Too late she saw the movement and tumbled into battle with a predator. Yipper her mind identified. She managed to scratch the soft underbelly and evade the near death grip on her throat.

Polana backed against the solid structure to protect her rear. She had to safeguard her kitten! She flattened her ears and hissed, tensing her body to spring. The yipper seemed to anticipate her move and lounged grabbing her throat.

She kicked her back claws marking her attacker. It held on and her eyes dimmed. Again she tried to free herself but she couldn't breathe and her body grew weak. Darkness dropped and in her last few heartbeats she heard a deep growl, a startled yelp and finally, nothing at all.

~ * ~

He was cold. He shivered rousing enough to wonder where his mother with his milk and her soothing purr were. Shakily he stumbled out onto the chill surface mewling for her.

He was hungry! He was cold! Surely she would come!

He cried louder his tiny heart pounding.

Hearing clicks he bounced clumsily toward the sound. She was coming! A strange unfamiliar scent reached his nose and he stopped. That didn't smell like his mother.

Backing away he bumped into something and froze. A long wet nose descended sniffing him. He shivered terrified and chilled. Where was his mother to protect him?

The nose lifted turning at a sound behind it. A strange sound came from its long mouth answered by another in the same manner. It came down to him again taking him into its mouth. Instinctively he relaxed as if his mother was carrying him.

Long dark ways blurred by. He entered a miserable world full of white and wet. He shivered uncontrollably and sneezed. Where was his mother? Who were these unknown creatures and why were they taking him away from her and the warm safe place she'd made for him?

He blinked his eyes as cold bit into his small body. He couldn't stop shaking. Another unknown creature nearby made a harsh sound. It laid down in the white and he was lowered to rest on warm though slightly wet fur.

It helped stop his shivering but too soon he was lifted again and taken even further away from his mother. He mewed and mewed for her to come until his throat ached. He sneezed and sneezed again.

He was hungry. He was cold. He was wet. Where was his mother?

Chapter 4

Tiny scrapes awakened me. I opened one eye and watched in amusement as the new kitten struggled to free a small bite of meat from the partially devoured goose. The piece abruptly tore sending the grey striped female into an ungraceful heap. She leapt up and pounced on the offending tidbit and started to gulp down her meal.

"Slowly. Or you'll throw up," Tomura warned.

The youngster slowed her eating. When she'd finished, she washed her face.

"What's your name?" my mate asked in her motherly tone. Her glance at me told me she knew I was awake. I knew though, some matters were best left to a female.

"Sasha." Her striking green eyes looked up. I noticed then the gold flecks floating near the iris.

"Welcome."

I opened my other eye and observed the two over my tail.

"My kittens are perhaps a half moon younger than you," Tomura went on.

"Really?!" Sasha bounded over and gazed into the nest. "I'll actually have someone to play with?"

She must have been an only kitten. Good. The two leg had only claimed one feline life.

Tomura rumbled her reassurance. "Yes."

Sasha glanced very shyly at me. "Thank you, for bringing me here."

"You're welcome," I responded, sitting up. She edged away from me. I could understand her fear. It is not usual for a male to bring the kitten of another to his den.

"You can stay with us until you're old enough to decide whether you want to stay or establish your own den and select your own mate." Tomura may think of this one as a potential mate, but I wanted the youngster to have a choice.

"Really?" Her round eyes widened. "Mama told me I wouldn't have a choice. I'd have to mate with whatever tom won..." she grew silent.

"What's wrong, Sasha?" Tomura asked.

"A big grey tom fathered me. He came to see me, but ran away when the two leg came." She paused. "It killed my mother."

"I asked Bast to reclaim her soul," I told her. "The two leg met Her judgment." I waited while she absorbed the news. "Do you know your father's name?"

"No." Sasha began to mew mournfully. "I miss my mother."

"Of course you do." Tomura consoled. "Come."

Sasha sheltered against my mate and yowled pitifully until she fell asleep.

A part of me hoped she'd accept me as her father.

~ * ~

Covertly, I watched the fight over the silver beauty. She hugged the stone wall as the two combatants struggled. One was Midnight, who I'd heard was expanding his territory farther than any other male ever had. The other was Mikki. I briefly thought about leaving if Mikki won. He and Starlite would produce strong kittens. But, I wanted this female for myself. She had the 'sight'.

Mikki yowled and cowered away. He hugged a wounded front paw to his gray chest.

"You yield," Midnight hissed.

In answer, the older male retreated.

The black tom faced me. My body tensed for battle.

"I'll have *this* one!" Midnight snarled.

"No. You won't," Starlite said.

Midnight leaped high making it easy for me to dodge under him. I'd been wise to arrive early and watch the tactics the other used to win his challenges. I whirled around, swatting him with my large paw. My sharp claws raked his face. He shrieked as if he were a female in heat.

"Half Breed," he taunted.

"My name is Word Warrior." I circled, seeking the advantage.

"Still a half breed. Still a mongrel."

"As are you."

The other tom breathed hard. He'd fought several matches before and since I'd arrived. He was tired. An advantage for me.

"I'm a Purebred Lart."

Bombay my mind automatically translated. "And yet you mate with those who aren't." My eyes watched his body. He had a slight limp. He was injured.

I darted in to grab his leg, but he anticipated my move and his claws sliced my hindquarters. I ignored the pain and bit down hard on his injured limb. He screamed yanking it away.

I felt blood dripping down my leg.

He lunged for my neck. I met him head on and caught his windpipe in my mouth. We tumbled to the ground.

"Yield," I hissed.

He tried to shake me loose. I held on putting more pressure on his throat. Midnight coughed and stopped struggling. Warily I released him. "Yield?"

Golden eyes blazed at me. "Yield," he conceded, violently twitching his tail. "There'll be another time Half Breed," he vowed as he limped away trailing blood.

"No doubt," I agreed, watching him leave. When I knew he'd gone, I began to wash my wounds.

"Allow me to help," Starlite said, her tongue joining mine in cleaning away the bitter blood.

Once the bleeding stopped and the wound was clean, I introduced myself. "I'm Word Warrior."

"I know," her stunning blue eyes met mine. She stood beside me poised, one paw daintily raised in the air. "You were destined to win me."

A sample of her 'sight'? Vaguely I recalled her comment to Midnight. She'd known he wouldn't win.

"You're destined for many things," she continued.

"Such as?"

"This is not the time." She rubbed against me. "I am your rightfully won prize, Word Warrior."

~ * ~

Starlite only looked back once in regret as we left the crumbling stone building she'd lived in. She hadn't really been surprised when I told her we would leave and go to my established den. She'd taken only a tinkling bell with her. "All I have of my mother," she'd explained.

As we crossed the snow covered plains for the school, she chattered happily. I wondered if she intended to talk the entire two-sunrise journey.

"You said Tomura approved of me coming."

"Yes. She encouraged me to win you."

"And you have how many kittens?"

"Seven. Plus a foundling."

"I'd heard you took in another male's kitten."

"It was right."

"Of course it was." She took a deep breath of crisp air. "How did you find it?"

"Starlite, it's a long story and we have a long ways to travel."

"Perfect for the telling of stories."

"I prefer to be silent."

"Most males do. My brother Algier liked quiet."

"I'll tell you the story when we stop to rest."

She twitched her tail but stopped asking questions until we crawled into a tree trunk for the night. It smelled faintly of fox. Starlite sneezed distastefully yet she made no objection to my choice of shelter. We curled together for warmth.

"Do you have an elder yet?" she asked as she pulled ice from between her toes.

"Not yet." I hadn't actually thought about adding one after my mother's refusal. Perhaps Tomura knew of an older feline. It would be her right to decide.

"My father's litter mate Callie might be a good choice. She raised my brother and I."

"Not your mother?"

"From what Callie told me, my mother mated with my father, had us, stayed a few moons and left. I don't even know her name."

Unusual behavior for a female. I couldn't recall a time when a mother had abandoned her kittens. "Where does Callie live?"

"In a deserted human dwelling in the low hills."

"Beginning of Hunter," I stopped myself. "Wolf territory."

"And butt sniffers. We used to have to hide from them constantly."

"I'll ask Tomura when we get to my den."

"She'll agree," Starlite responded. "I know Callie would want to come and live with me. She hates the hunt…wolves."

~ * ~

I made the ten-sunrise journey reluctantly. Tomura had agreed with my new female. We needed an Elder and she didn't argue when Starlite suggested Callie. "None of my blood would come," my mate told me. I knew her lowered status was why.

Fortunately, a rare break in the storms accompanied me though it made it more difficult for me to elude the dogs. I'd crossed the trail of many and had to detour around constantly so I wouldn't be seen. I slid across thick ice patches in an attempt to hide my scent as well. I also caught glimpses of a wolf female. Again, I wondered why the canine would roam so far from their normal territory.

I paused, my tail swishing slightly, sniffing the brisk wind. The tangy scent of an approaching storm strongly announced itself. I'd have to hurry. My hope had been to return to the school with our new Elder before the next snow. The weather however appeared as if it wasn't going to co-operate.

Bounding past a collapsed church, I cleared ice-covered timbers and brushed my back against long icicles. Starlite's more detailed directions, which she'd given me just before I left, indicated Callie lived in the basement of an old human apartment complex. As the light began to dim I saw the leaning tall buildings and thanked the Provider my destination loomed near.

Sliding under a snapped board I plunged into near dark. I waited as my eyes adjusted and cautiously crept down steep, creaky steps. I hoped they wouldn't fall and trap me in this dismal place. My feet touched the very cold, slippery floor. Gingerly I crossed it until I came to a smaller room. Several machines lined the wall and some stood in the center. Pictures in books identified them as washers and dryers. Starlite had told me Callie lived here.

"Callie?" I called.

"Go away," a cranky voice answered. "I'm too old to have kittens."

"I come with a message from Starlite. She wishes you to join us as our Elder."

Two bright sun yellow eyes appeared. "Why would a male do her bidding?" she snapped.

"I'm not like other males. I stay with my females and help raise our kittens. Besides, my first female agreed you were the best choice."

"I've heard stories." She poked her orange head out looking down at me from the dryer above. "About a male who reads. Who took in a kitten not his own."

"My name is Word Warrior. The stories are true."

"Won my Starlite in challenge did you?"

"She knew I would."

"Rare talent. Like her mother," she said so softly I almost didn't hear her.

"One of the reasons I fought for her."

"Bet you bested Midnight."

How had she guessed?

She snorted, landing on the floor with a thunk. "That one is too ambitious for his own good. Runt of his litter says rumor. Trying to prove his worth to a mother who really doesn't care."

"My mother is the same."

"They're the foolish ones. You've done well." She headed for the door. "We can make the old human shopping place before full nightfall."

"A storm is coming." I ran to catch up with her.

"Not before moonrise. Night is the best time to evade the sniffers and the hunters."

"Agreed."

Together we ascended the stairs, which swayed under our paws. Reaching the top Callie took the lead and we ran across the high drifts. Night fell with the wind picking up and tossing loose snow in our eyes. Thunder rolled across the sky.

"Thunder snow," Callie commented.

I remembered a few times when it had happened. A rare occurrence. Glancing behind us, I noticed the heavy snow filled clouds settle low on the hills. A few flakes fell swirling onto the white landscape.

"There's a tunnel ahead. We'll reach the old shopping place, mall, I think they called it, that way." Following her I entered the passage. It was larger than the one around our school. Any dog or wolf could use it as well. In fact, lingering smells indicated they had. The distance went on for a long way, narrowing to just cat size. I scraped through, knowing I'd have to have a long wash when we finally reached our destination.

"We're there," Callie's voice echoed back.

I emerged into a large open area. Wilted trees stood naked, their brittle leaves littering the floor. Shattered glass spread everywhere on the light colored floor. Carefully we picked our way through. Callie leaped up on an old wooden table.

"There's a place we can sleep." She jumped again.

The place must have been an old furniture store. Human sized clocks, chairs, tables, and other assorted things lay everywhere. Some were intact but others had been smashed. I followed her to a ripped up bed. Already she was bathing herself and settling in for the dark. I did the same.

As I washed I observed Callie must have been a beauty in her day. She had the fine markings of an orange Tabby. The only marr on her face was a deep scar. I finished washing and wondered where we might find a fat rat to feast on.

Almost, as if she read my mind she said, "Plenty of rats living at the other end. We won't starve if the storm traps us here for a moon."

I rose and circled several times. I needed to warm myself and sleep before hunting. I huddled into a tight ball.

Callie rested her head on her front paws. "Starlite's mother had the 'sight' you know."

With a sigh, I shrugged off sleep to listen.

"Said once she could hear the humans lamenting."

Now at least, I knew where Starlite got her chattiness from. "Did she say what she heard?'

"No." Confusion flickered in her eyes. "She'd say odd things about hearing them and then go on with stories like she'd been here before the long winter."

"Strange female."

"Yes," Callie lifted her head. "In other ways, too. Her coloring I'd never seen before and she spoke as if, well, as if she too could read."

Was that possible? Had there been one before me who could read?

"She'd tell stories about a world with three moons where her people danced under their light and held matings."

"The books I've read talk about other planets in our solar system. None of them could support life though."

"I always thought her mad. But her stories were entertaining and helped pass the long nights."

"Did her 'sight' do that to her?" Concern for Starlite and the welfare of our future kittens troubled me.

"I don't know." Callie lay her head down again and yawned. She had a few broken teeth and her breath stank. "I'm going to sleep now."

Good. I closed my eyes and dreamed of a world far away—full of rodents, birds, and other trinkets cats adored. I awoke to Callie's insistent nip on my paw.

"Go hunt. I'm hungry," she demanded.

Slowly rising, I stretched. First, I'd have to find a spot to relieve myself. Afterward, I'd go hunting rat. Returning later, I laid the dead rodent before her. Callie ate her fill and I finished off the rest.

"Still snowing. We won't be able to travel." The older female took a break from washing her face. "There aren't any tunnels that go through either."

I'd have to trust her knowledge. I had never traveled this far. I jumped off the bed and looked around. "I'm going to explore."

"If you want." She curled up. "I'm going to sleep."

I left Callie and wandered out into the old human mall. If we had to stay here for awhile, I might as well see what I could find. Being watchful not to step on glass, I found a metal staircase. I climbed up discovering much to my delight, a place full of books.

Slipping through the door, I explored the shelves. Many of the books were missing. There were odd signs – Religion – Business – Local Travel – Computers – Fiction. I found a couple high up and knocked them to the floor. Prying open the pages I spent the sunrise reading about the ancient world.

When the outside windows grew dark, I stopped and went back downstairs to Callie. She still slept. I hunted rat again, killing two this time. I wanted to spend more time reading tomorrow and didn't want to have stop and hunt. I put the rats on top of a table for later.

We spent three sunrises in the mall before the storm lifted. Regretfully I left my place of books to continue the journey. Maybe later I could return and read more. Callie led for awhile surrendering her place to me when she no longer knew the territory.

Luckily, we didn't cross any dog trails. They were probably holed up somewhere and would wait until later to go out. I thought this a good thing. I did pick up wolf scent, but it was never strong.

Several sunrises later we trudged into the school. Starlite greeted Callie warmly and showed the new Elder the place they'd prepared for her. The older female liked it. My two females had given Callie a smaller room to herself and they'd shredded an old rug for her to sleep on.

Tomura helped me dry myself and she shared with me a rat she'd caught earlier. My mate entertained me with stories of the antics of the kittens, including their reaction to being part of their first hunt.

"They didn't catch anything. It was more fun for them to just chase the scurriers…rats."

I purred my approval as my kittens climbed all over me welcoming me home. They finally fell asleep in a warm pile around me.

Chapter 5

The lone howler cry caused Anumati to raise her huge white, black spotted head. Anxiously her pale green eyes surveyed her three very small cubs. She'd been lucky to find this cave and ready it for the arrival of her young. She'd dragged in broken boughs of the soft needled trees, shaking them to free the branches from the clinging snow.

Her cubs slept for now, secure and warm by her side. Carefully, she moved, so not to disturb them and padded to the slightly sheltered entrance. Battered wood hung at a strange angle, keeping the worst of the heavy storm out.

Blinding white fell, obscuring the few trees that had survived the ravages of the endless winter. Anumati listened for the howl again, hearing an echoing answer. She wasn't afraid of the cunning canines, her claw and fangs were more than a match for them, but she was nervous about a pack being so close to her chosen den.

Silence fell. She waited. When no more howler calls replied to each other, she allowed herself to relax and returned to her cubs. Her tongue cleaned each and they nursed eagerly. Quietly they growled at each other before they settled down to sleep again.

Anumati proudly rested. She'd birthed two females and one male. She would wait many sunrises and sets before naming them. Her kind believed names were symbolic, her own meant 'moon' because she'd been birthed during a full moon. Care was taken in a naming and she needed to see what traits or talents her cubs displayed first.

Closing her eyes she prepared to nap, when faint scratching reached her ears. Alert, yet pretending she didn't hear it, her ears pricked forward, attentive for the noise again. It didn't sound like a large foot or a lost horned one. More like claws on rock.

Her eyes opened to mere slits to watch. Two faint shadows were on the rock. Her nose tried to pick up the scent. She desperately wanted to open her mouth to know the intruders smell.

The two shadows entered her den. Howlers! Her muscular body went taut. Anumati prepared for battle, yet the invaders sat down, blinking sky blue eyes at her. She noticed the white hanging from one of their mouths. Perhaps they had simply come to eat their prey and depart or share the cave warmth for the night. Such had happened before.

The howler holding the white rose taking a few steps toward her. She growled a warning. It stopped placing the white mound on the ground. The canine whined, pushing at the lump with its pointed nose.

Curiosity at their strange behavior won out and she got up, keeping her body between the howlers and her cubs. The howler moved back, sitting beside the other. They watched her with eager eyes.

Carefully she sniffed at the fur. Expecting a large foot she was surprised to find the familiar odor of feline, despite the smell of howler. She licked the tiny body. It mewed and moved its legs.

The howler barked what she took for encouragement. Somehow, she got the feeling if they had wanted the small feline dead, they would have killed it and ate it already. Why had they brought it to her?

She took the body in her mouth, taking great care not to crush it, and backed onto the boughs. She put the tiny feline beside her, cleaned it, and tried to figure out how she was going to get some milk into it.

The howlers both barked. Startled, she looked at them. They got to their huge paws and trotted out. Vaguely she wondered if they actually knew what they were doing or had simply surrendered their intended prey to her.

Desperate mews distracted her and she knew she had to find a way to feed the hungry tiny cub. Finally, she managed to draw some of her milk from her own tit and dribbled the liquid into the mouth of her new charge. When it had its fill, it fell asleep, a tiny lump of warmth at her side.

How had her foundling managed to become separated from its mother and why had the howlers really brought it to her? She laid her head on her large paws. Somehow, she doubted she'd ever discover the answers.

~ * ~

"Come," I ordered my bouncy brood. They all raced after me into the room filled with books. Library, it was called. I propped open an old primer against the chair leg. Sasha took a place beside my first born male. She seemed unsure, as if she thought I'd object to her being here.

"A," I boomed, bumping the letter on the book.

"A," my seven kittens repeated.

"A," Sasha's trembling voice alone.

I tried to encourage Sasha with an approving purr. She looked away.

"B,"

"B," all eight spoke together.

I turned to the next page, taking care not to rip the page. There was no way we could replace the precious contents.

"C,"

"C,"

Maybe Tomura's suggestion held merit. Perhaps Sasha would make an excellent future mate. Still, I had promised her a chance to choose. I had no intention of taking that away from her.

"D,"

~ * ~

A very large female Trixia as they called themselves or Maine Coon, as I knew they'd once been called, strolled into our den. She was all black with a white chest and matching paws. Tomura hissed and her kittens ran to the nest to hide in the rags. Starlite, heavy with her own, snarled at the newcomer.

"I am Lara," she announced. "I've come to mate with Word Warrior."

I could smell her strong scent. The new female was in heat. Forcing myself to sit down, despite the wild desire to mount her, I said coldly, "I don't mate with just any female."

"Nor would I allow him to!" Tomura landed in front of me, her short bronze fur fluffed. I knew my mate would stand her ground and not allow the new female, nor myself, to proceed with any type of mating without her permission.

Lara cocked her head to one side. "I haven't come all this way and fought off other toms to waste time fighting with you."

My mate spat. "You impertinent…"

"Why have you come?" Starlite's soft voice broke into the tension filled room.

Round copper eyes, glinting with sly knowledge regarded my second mate. "I've heard you have the 'sight'. You tell me."

The sleek silver beauty waddled over to stand beside Tomura. "You have something to offer us."

She snorted. "Obvious."

"Then tell us the obvious," I demanded.

Lara's long fluffy tail jerked. "Maybe I'll just leave."

"No," Starlite objected. "What you know, we would not want another tom to gain."

"Why don't you just stop with the word talk and spit it out," Callie interjected. "All this fuss over nothing," our Elder huffed as she sat glaring at us all.

"What have you come to share with us?" I asked more gently.

She pulled herself up proudly. "I know numbers."

My eyes widened in surprise. Tomura gasped. Starlite nodded knowingly and retreated to the nest where my kittens hid. Callie made a lisping noise through her broken teeth.

"I can also do math. Taught myself."

Much as I prided myself on my reading skills, the mystery of numbers and how they related to each other still eluded me. Two of my kittens, Mattie and Fern, had been demanding to learn and I couldn't teach them.

"Do you understand how the humans used math?" Her reply would dictate whether or not I accepted her. If she lied, I'd allow Tomura to chase her off.

"I struggled. At first. It took many moonrises to unravel addition and subtraction. Once I understood those, I went on to figure out how to multiply and divide."

"Really?" Tiny Fern hurried over. "Can you teach me?"

Tomura moved to grab her kitten. Lara tensed.

"I'm not a rival male who would harm your kitten."

My mate paused, her tail twitching. "No. You aren't," she agreed, backing off, while still glowering at the other female.

"She has much to offer us, Tomura," Starlite put in. "We should welcome Lara."

"I wish to approve all your females," she returned. I knew she wanted me to reinforce her position as my dominate mate.

Her haughty possessive attitude irritated me. I swatted at her. She dodged my paw.

"*I* decide which females I mate with. As my head female, you're privileged. But *don't* overstep your place!"

Her chocolate eyes flamed, like an old house I'd seen burn down once. I thought briefly she might strike at me and I readied myself to fight with her.

"He's right," Callie informed Tomura. "We females have some rights, but the males chose whom they want. You should know that."

My head female spared the Elder a glance. "I bow to your wisdom." Her body stance informed me she spoke only words.

"Good. Now." Callie strolled over beside Lara. "Let's get you cleaned up, fed, and rested before you join Word Warrior in mating." Her wise old eyes met Tomura's. "I want more kittens to tell my tales to."

~ * ~

Starlite produced a small litter of two brown and black mottled males and a silver-white female. I stood beside her nest examining the tiny bodies. Three more! Three more who would learn to read and hopefully understand math. Three more to help change the destiny of felines!

My happiness and pride proved to be short lived. One of the males died during the dark. Starlite couldn't bring herself to do the proper thing by eating its body, so I took it outside and found a deep hole to drop it down. Muttering a prayer to Bast asking for the safe flight of its soul, I returned to my female to share her mourning.

I mated with Lara watching with satisfaction as her belly grew heavy. She told me she doubted there would be more than two or three, yet that didn't matter to me. I knew I would mate many times with my females and we would raise many kittens.

Lara began teaching math. Only four of my kittens showed an aptitude for numbers, Mattie, Fern, Chev and Maurie. They spent many sunrises pouring over figures and excitedly telling their siblings about it.

Tomura began to take her kittens on hunting trips. Starlite's two wanted to join in, but their mother, much to my amusement, told them they were still too young to begin stalking rat. I occasionally distance hunted, hoping to vary our diet from the constant rodent with a catch of rabbit or goose or perhaps the wily rodent called a squirrel.

Still, I began to worry. Stories from the other males told me Midnight had a huge territory, and I sniffed his urine—sprayed closer and closer to my den. I feared to return and find my kittens slaughtered and my females claimed!

~ * ~

Callie held court in her small room. All my kittens gathered around her, scampering excitedly. My females lay on old rugs, enjoying some peace, while our Elder tried to get my young to settle down.

"If you want to hear a story," she boomed, "you have to settle down. Otherwise, you'll go to sleep without one."

Her threat of no story seemed to get their attention. Some sprawled on each other, while others nuzzled beside their mothers, and a couple sat next to me.

"Tonight," Callie paused to wash a spot on her face with her paw, "I will share something my Starlite's mother quoted. Not sure where she got it from."

Maurie and Poppin were batting at each other. Callie swatted at them and they stopped.

"Now listen," she instructed.

*"Lilacs once loomed
over the weathered fence
where our dog dug holes
and our cat chased butterflies.*

*Trees hung heavy with
golden delicious apples
small tastes taken by birds
and picked by squirrels
to hide away for winter's sting."*

"What are lilacs?" Poppin asked. He'd ended up a plain brown and had inherited my turquoise eyes.

"Shhh," his sister Sheila replied. "I want to listen." She shared her brother's brown coloring, but her head and paws were black. She'd gotten her almond shaped chocolate eyes from her mother.

Callie continued.

*"Huge orange pumpkins
for carving scary faces,
long dark green zucchini
for bread and frying,
carrots for lunch snacks
and our rabbit,
who we ate
last week.*

All covered now
white thick with
still falling flakes.
Winter's bitter bite
for unknown
number of years."

"What's a pumpkin?" Chev wanted to know. He blinked his green eyes and stretched his growing black body with his mother's bronze head and tail. "And why carve scary faces? And what's zucchini? And what…"

"Vegetables humans grew once," I answered.

"The humans had a holiday they called Halloween," Callie added. "Some sort of ritual."

"Will we find out more about Hall…o…ween?" Neutron questioned, his golden brown eyes looking up at me. He cleaned a spot on his brown and black mottled shoulder.

"We might." I hadn't thought of trying to find anything on past human events. I was more interested in learning to read their language, not actually understand why they did anything. Though, I had gleaned some things about their culture.

"What's that noise?" Sapphire jumped up on the narrow windowsill and gazed out.

Rumbling shook the chilled floor. Everyone sat up, ears straight and listening, bodies tense, ready to flee.

I jumped up to join my kitten. She moved her silver-white body to give me more room. Gazing out on the dark landscape, I saw two bright dots pierce the dark.

My protective instincts kicked in. "Get everyone safely to your nests! Now!"

Sapphire jumped down and joined her mother Starlite and her brother Neutron. Tomura gathered her seven and Sasha. Silently they hurried to the other room.

Callie joined me. "Looks like the picture of the human cars."

"Sort of." The odd box shape rolled past the school. It didn't resemble any of the pictures I'd seen in the books with its huge metal teeth rolling over the deep snow.

"You don't suppose they'll come in here?" Callie actually sounded frightened.

"You think there are humans in it?" The idea made me uncomfortable. I thought of humans as past masters, now gone. Surely none of them had survived and now returned in metal monsters!

"We don't know what happened to them all." She peered closer. "Maybe you should follow it and find out."

It was a thought. I watched the metal monster crawl away. Should I follow and discover what type of creatures created such a machine?

Chapter 6

I tumbled end over end with my rival. We hissed at each other and yowled, circling, each trying to find the advantage over the other. Midnight flicked his tail and lunged. I barely managed to escape his teeth as he tried for my throat.

Unfortunately, the black tom wasn't exhausted this time. There hadn't been many competitors for Mitzy and I vaguely wondered why. She seemed to be a healthy Calico, with a shapely spotted head, and matching splotches of orange and black over her white petite body.

Midnight jumped at me. I dodged and tried to pounce on him. My wily competitor squirmed and escaped my attempt to grab his throat. We both crouched issuing battle cries. I noticed his blood encrusted ear.

I darted to the side and chomped on his ear surprised he didn't remember my tactic from our last challenge. He yowled and pulled away. Blood dripped down his scarred face. I tried to leap again but something large slobbered on the black male.

Midnight screeched, whirled, and raced out of the old firehouse. Breathing hard, I slowly backed up as the small wolf pranced playfully.

"Jojo," Mitzy called. "Bad."

The canine whined and lay down, its silver-black head resting on huge paws.

The sleek Calico blinked her round yellow-brown eyes. She trotted over to the wolf and gave it an affectionate lick. The young wolf tried to leap at her, but she swatted its nose. A yip escaped the large mouth and it hunkered down, pressing its belly against the floor whining.

"Jojo is really harmless," she said.

"Where did you get the wolf, hunter," I searched for the word. I'd seen it in a human book on animals. "Cub?"

"I found him outside just after I lost my first batch of kittens. Have no idea where he came from."

"Any of his pack come looking for him?" I couldn't imagine the cub being left in the care of a feline.

"One of the females leaves food for him. He's too big to nurse now."

She daintily licked her paw and rubbed at a spot on her muzzle. "She's never tried to take him away."

Odd. I'd talked with many of the other males. There was a wolf pack living in the old city. Yet, there were also many stories being told of the wolves helping felines and not hunting us as they once had.

"I'm raising him," Mitzy went on. "You've won me in challenge. And Jojo comes with me."

Callie hated the wolves. I had no idea what her reaction might be. "My Elder doesn't like them."

"Jojo's harmless," Mitzy repeated.

~ * ~

Another high mountain storm had blown in during the dark. Anumati paced restlessly. Not only did she need to hunt, but she also wanted to see Sanjiv. The very old one was known for his wisdom and knowledge. She hoped he could help her.

She'd managed to keep feeding her foundling, yet he didn't seem to be thriving. He no longer mewed and kept scratching at his ears. His nose was dry and he hacked constantly. She feared he would die.

The lives of felines were few and precious. She couldn't allow the gift given her to perish. With a final check on her cubs, all of whom lay in tight balls and together, she made a decision. She would brave the snow. Her ball of snow fur, that might be a good name for her foundling she mused, needed help. She could not wait for the storm to end.

Lastly, she checked the small feline. After killing a large foot on a previous hunt, she'd used the fur to help keep him warm. He lay safe and some distance from her cubs. She didn't want them crushing him. He hacked and shook. Instinctively, she knew she didn't have much time. If she wanted him to live, she had to leave. Now.

Leaping out into the snow, she relied on her instincts. Keeping her great head down to protect her eyes from blinding snow, she pushed through the deepening drifts. Sanjiv didn't den far from her. She was grateful for that.

Cold grabbed her in its claws. Shivering, determined, she made the journey and stumbled into his den finally. She dried herself quickly, and padded further inside. Sanjiv slept. His great white mound with faded black spots breathed slowly on the hide of a horned one.

"Sanjiv," she whispered reverently.

He snorted, raising his head to stare blindly at her. "Who comes?"

"I am Anumati," she identified herself. "I have an ill cub."

"What symptoms does it have?"

"I don't understand."

"How can you tell it is ill?"

"It, he, Snow Fur, rubs at his ears, his nose is dry and he hacks when he breathes."

"Not one of our traditional names."

"The howlers brought him to me. He is feline, but not one of us."

"One of the valley felines then. Cats they're called."

"What can I do? I fear he will soon die."

The old one absently scratched his neck. "All I can suggest is bark."

"Bark?"

"Yes. From the pines. Strip the outside and chew the inside. Make it thin, like your milk and feed it to your, Snow Fur, did you call him?"

"I did."

"He'll either live or die. Sekhmet will decide."

"Thank you, Sanjiv. Is there anything you need?" she offered out of respect.

The old one considered. "Perhaps, when next you hunt, you could bring me a large foot. I would like that."

"I will find you one," Anumati promised as she left.

On her way back to her den, she broke a pine branch and dragged it through the drifts to her den. Once back inside, she again dried herself and set about following the instructions the wise one had given her.

Chewing the bitter tasting stuff she didn't like. She ground the bark into a liquid with her teeth and forced the mixture into Snow Fur's mouth. She even licked some of it around his ears. She tucked his tiny form between her paws as her cubs nursed. She needed to keep him warm.

She bathed her cubs and they settled around her to sleep. Anumati breathed a prayer to Sekhmet for the healing of Snow Fur hoping the fierce goddess would be merciful.

~ * ~

"What is that hunter doing here?" Callie screamed arching her back.

"Callie," I growled. "Mitzy's cub is no danger to us."

Our Elder hissed at the playful antics of the cub. My kittens had scattered, hiding behind busted timbers and furniture.

Tiny Nan crept back out curious about the young wolf. "Where'd he come from, Daddy?" Nan, whose appearance was so like Tomura's, except her eyes were yellow, had always been the first to try new things.

"He was left at my door," Mitzy explained. "I'm raising him."

"Felines don't' raise howlers!" Callie snorted.

Sasha dashed in disrupting our introduction. "Come see Lara's kittens!"

Mitzy stood protectively near Jojo, her fur fluffed. Callie's tail flipped displaying her anger. I stepped between my new mate and our Elder. "Enough!"

"Making a mistake…accepting this…creature!"

"I'm accepting him just as I did Sasha…and you."

Callie hissed again and retreated back to her room. She paused at the doorway, "See if I tell stories to *her* kittens!"

I joined Sasha, my mates, and my excited youngsters around Lara's nest. My large Maine Coon mate had made herself at home in one of the other rooms and managed to find thick wool to have her kittens on. Three small fluffs of fur squirmed beside her.

"All male," Lara tiredly informed me. "I've named them Trotsky, Stirling, and Hardy."

Truthfully, I don't resent my females naming their own kittens, although, there were times when I wished they'd ask me what names I might like.

Mitzy shyly approached. Tomura and Starlite warmly greeted her with welcoming purrs. Lara had already fallen asleep. Jojo bounced into the room. Mitzy headed him off with a nip on his paw. He yipped, escaped to the door, and waited there.

"You've trained him well," Tomura observed warily watching the cub.

"Well, he is rather large. I didn't want him stepping on me and certainly not on any of the kittens."

"Will he play with me?" Nan wanted to know. She skittishly approached him, drawing back, and moved toward him again.

He cocked his head at her, his long pink tongue dripping on the dusty floor, and tail wagging, causing a small storm behind him.

Nan jumped at him. Jojo barked. My kitten danced between his large feet and the two dashed down the hall in a game of chase.

"At least he'll have someone to play with," Mitzy observed.

Tomura ran to the door and watched the game. I could tell she was concerned about our tiny kitten. The wolf and Nan went past, Jojo gently pushing her along on the floor with his long nose.

"Hi, mama," Nan shouted gleefully.

"Jojo won't hurt your kitten," Mitzy reassured my first female.

"He had better not," Tomura replied, her chocolate eyes blazing a warning. "I would take his eyes and leave him out in the snow."

~ * ~

Mitzy gave birth adding four more kittens to my growing brood. She decided to call the three females, Kara, Ulma, and Izzy. The only male she named Clomper. "I like simple names," she told me.

Jojo, when he met my new mate's kittens promptly adopted them. When I'd pass by to check on them, I often saw the wolf cub bathing them, or keeping them warm when Mitzy needed a break.

Secretly, I was glad she had relief help. My other females had accepted Mitzy. Their main prejudice focused on the wolf cub who constantly followed her. As a result they hadn't offered to watch her kittens or invite her to join the rat hunts.

Our Elder, Callie, still refused to have anything to do with Mitzy. The old female gladly told stories to the other kittens. Yet every chance she had she reminded my new mate *her* kittens were not welcome nor would they ever be.

~ * ~

I had kept watch for the odd machine that had passed by. I'd taken time to follow the irregular tracks a half-sunrise distance. When I'd returned, I'd found pieces of deer outside our door smelling very strongly of wolf. I remembered Mitzy mentioning one of the females leaving food for the cub. They must have finally figured out where he was.

I was uncomfortable with the idea and searched several body lengths away to see if they were denned close by. I found no trace and told Mitzy about the food. She had Jojo go pull it inside. The cub growled when we tried to share the meat. Nan crawled beside him and took a bite and he seemed to accept her presence.

Once he finished his meal and had gone to take a nap we all dined on deer meat. The tasty fair was a welcome relief from the constant rat diet. Even Callie accepted a choice morsel with no complaint.

At the rate the wolf was growing, I knew at some point the cub would have to leave and join a pack. I hadn't discussed his fate with Mitzy yet, she considered him to be her own kitten. He played well with Nan, and I had noticed she often slept securely between his large paws.

I mused over this as I kneaded the old wool I slept on. Tomorrow another male gathering was planned and I needed to be traveling just before the sun rose. The journey would be short, to the old mall just past the crumbling fire station. I wanted to get there early to discover if any other tom had seen the strange machine.

~ * ~

I entered the mall. We would be gathering by the huge fireplace. Odd, how I more and more called structures and objects the same as the humans. The influence of my reading about them increased every day.

Slowly wandering over the old stone floor, I paused. Many of the other toms were already there and I thought I'd heard my name.

"Word Warrior allows his females too much freedom."

I silently walked closer, using the broken furniture as cover, not wanting to be seen. Sneaking a glance over a fallen timber I noticed for the first time the decorative metal grates, which hung crookedly on the hinges. Crouching back down, I rested my belly on cold rock. My ears twitched as I listened.

"Did you hear what happened with a female Midnight tried to rightfully claim?" another male asked. I didn't know him and wondered if he was a young male from a local female or a tom looking for new territory.

"No," my old friend Mikki answered.

"When he came to kill her kittens by another tom so he could mate with her himself, she battled with him and said he should learn by Word Warrior's deeds and just accept them as his own!"

Several toms hissed and yowled in protest.

"If other females learn of this," Mikki began concerned.

"They'll have no respect for us, the natural order of proper mating rules, or the Right of Challenge," Talhal agreed.

"All because," the stranger went on, "Word Warrior took a kitten not his own. Not to mention a high hunter!"

More hisses and yowls followed his statement. My muscles contracted between my shoulders. Had my desire for a new feline destiny and following the wisdom I learned from the humans, now separated me from my fellow toms?

"So what defiant female dared to stop Midnight?" Talhal inquired angrily.

"Her name is Dia. She lives in the old stump close to the best hopper hunting."

Not far from the school or the old mall. Quietly I slipped out, using the rubble to hide myself, and headed back into the snow. The sun rose across the vast white plain making tiny sparkles ripple over the drifts. Finding the female's den would not be difficult. Whether or not she'd let me near it and her kittens, however, concerned me.

I leapt through the fresh powder, left from a recent storm, rejoicing in the crisp air and the rarity of a non-snow day. Skidding down the hill I crossed the small distance before going under what used to be a highway overpass. The broken and cracked chunks of concrete and steel stared at me like cleaned rat bones.

Continuing across the plain I debated on catching a fine hopper, or rabbit as the humans once called them. Perhaps an offering of food would soften Dia's heart. But, if she lived near the best hunting spot, no doubt she would be tired of them.

One of the rabbits darted across my path. Instinctively I wanted to chase it. My body tensed in excitement. A nice tasty hopper would be a welcome change, even with the occasional addition of deer meat we enjoyed. Slinking down I used a slight rise as cover as my prey nibbled at something just sticking out of the snow.

Its twitching nose detected me and the rabbit darted behind a rock. I dashed after it only to discover it had taken refuge in a deep hole. Pushing my huge head in, my whiskers alerted me it was too small for my entire body. Disappointed, I turned away and plodded through the drifts slowing as I neared the stump I was certain Dia lived in. Sniffing carefully, I didn't detect the strong scent of Midnight's urine, instead…I stopped, alert, ducking behind another clump of skeleton trees. Out of the stump the white head of a wolf appeared. The canine scanned the area and pulled back in.

Had a wolf taken over the female's den? I crept slowly forward, my belly brushing the cold damp snow. Cautiously I peaked inside, starting, at what I saw. The wolf lay on the nest, two kittens safely tucked at its furry white side.

Clear blue eyes met mine. The wolf barked softly. Sensing an invitation, I entered. The canine whined as the kittens mewed. Somehow, I seemed to know the two were hungry.

And I wondered, what had become of their mother?

I left the stump and used my nose to find any unfamiliar scent. There was a feline trace, probably Dia, and not far away two deep tracks of the metal monster.

My tail twitched. Had the female been taken away by whatever had built the machine? Or had she been killed as rightful prey? I had no way of knowing, but the wolf protecting the kittens told me Dia would not be returning.

I re-entered the stump and picked up the closest kitten by the neck, still uneasy at what the wolf's reaction might be. Mitzy had just had hers and I had no doubt she would nurse these two. I'd take the crying kitten to her and return for the second, if the wolf allowed me to take them. Cautiously stepping back outside watching the reaction of the canine, I was surprised to find the wolf had picked up the other and followed. I hesitated. The canine whined again.

Turning toward home and very uneasy at the wolf's behavior, despite the help I'd gotten from another of its kind, I hurried trying to keep the exposure to the minimum in order to insure the survival of my newest foundlings. Around the crumbled houses and up the hill to the school, I entered using the old buckled door, sparing a backward look at the wolf who was still there.

The wolf's nails clicked on the tile floor. Curious kittens scampered out and dashed back out of sight. Their soft cries to their mothers alerted them to the intrusion. Tomura stood at one door; her attractive back arched, ears back, a high pitched yowl filling the dark hall.

With the kitten in my mouth, I couldn't tell her to be silent, so I hastened my pace and walked into the room where Mitzy made her nest. I put the black kitten in her nest. The wolf gently deposited the gray one and barked, answered by the same in a tone I realized was not Jojo's.

Laying less than a body length away, was a large black and gray wolf. The one who had come with me cowered away and laid down several body lengths away.

"Word Warrior, meet the dominate female Lavena. The other who came with you is the lowest female Rowena." Mitzy gazed wonderingly at me. "Where did you get these kittens?"

"They're Dia's." I quickly explained what I'd overheard at the male gathering and finding the wolf at the stump. "I don't know where their mother is," I finished.

"Poor dears." Mitzy promptly washed them and urged them to nurse.

The dominate female woofed. Mitzy listened intently. "She says the mother went hunting and didn't return. They decided Rowena would stay to keep them warm while the males went searching."

"You understand the wolves?" I didn't remember my latest mate mentioning she could do that, but if she could, maybe I could find out why the wolves had been behaving so strangely.

"Well, of course. How else do you think Jojo and I communicate?" Her tone sounded offended.

It had never occurred to me she spoke with Jojo in a manner other than our own language. I kept silent, not wishing to show my lack of understanding over such a simple concept, nor my great surprise.

Lavena barked again. Mitzy translated. "She says she's hearing stories from the high peak packs and from her sister pack about finding a kitten of a slain female." She paused as Lavena continued. "No! That can't be true!"

Chapter 7

Snow Fur no longer shivered and Anumati began to relax. Maybe he would survive after all. She had managed to get a little milk into him earlier. He hacked again, but not as hard as before. She'd keep giving him some of the chewed up bark for a couple more sunrises. Later, she'd have to go hunt a large foot and deliver it to Sanjiv as her thanks for his wisdom.

Her three cubs tumbled on the cold dirt. They were growing fast. She'd finally settled on names for them. Her son she'd call Valmiki and her two daughters Jyotis and Kerani. She'd present them to Sekhmet after they made their first kill and would teach them how to leave the goddess a blood offering.

But that was many moons away. She would need to care for and instruct them for now. There was much to learn in this land of snow and storms. Where to den. How to hunt. When to mate.

Her foundling kicked his tiny legs. Raising him would be a challenge. Anumati would not be able to use the same skills her mother taught her in the raising of cubs. He was too small to hunt the horned ones. Perhaps she could teach him to hunt large foot. She hoped he would grow big enough to kill one.

Her cubs bounded over to the entrance. The recent storm had piled mounds at the entrance. The three took turns putting their oversize paws on it and bouncing away, then testing the damp cold again.

Amused at their play, she laid her head down. She hadn't slept much and she needed to rest. Caring for her sick foundling had kept her up for many long darks. She knew she'd have to wait until her cubs tired and hoped she could nap when they did.

Soon they tired and fought with each other for the spot nearest her. Tumbled together they fell asleep. Anumati checked on Snow Fur, keeping him close to warm him. He sneezed though his breathing sounded better. Protectively she cradled him between her paws and took her earned nap.

~ * ~

She presented Sanjiv with the large foot she'd caught earlier. The old one inspected her offering with a long sniff. He pulled the meat to him and began to work the skin loose.

"Thank you," she said.

He gulped down a bite. "A nice young one. Tender." He tore off another choice bit, chewed and swallowed. "Your Snow Fur is recovered then?"

"Yes. What you told me about the bark helped him."

"Hmmm." He ate more. "One thing you might want to consider, Anumati."

"What is that?"

"He is a valley feline and may not survive the high places. Perhaps, just perhaps, you should consider returning him below."

A cold fear touched her not unlike the winds. "He was brought to me for a purpose."

"I agree." He licked blood from his paw. "I was not suggesting trying to find his mother."

"What then?" His words confused her.

"There are stories coming to us from the valley. Stories of a feline who can read. Who took in kittens not his own."

Was he suggesting what she thought? "You wish me to take Snow Fur to this feline who can read?"

"It is only a thought. As his mother, even adopted, you must always consider what is best for Snow Fur."

~ * ~

"Did they kill it?" I asked, fear for the safety of my kittens filling me.

"No. They didn't kill him. They took him to one of the Spotted Ghosts."

"The Spotted Ghosts?" I couldn't believe it. They were only stories!

"The packs that live high in the mountains see them sometimes." Mitzy washed her new two kittens again, making certain they were close beside her and warm.

"Mitzy," something else the female had said bothered me. "Lavena said there was a sister pack. How many wolves live in the valley now?"

Mitzy gruffly hacked. Lavena answered.

"Only three. The other two are packs established by two of her daughters. And Word Warrior." I met her yellow-brown eyes. "She says they lost a cub when that metal monster rolled through."

"Why should we care?" Tomura asked from the doorway, her thin tail swishing angrily.

"And if it had been one of your kittens?" Mitzy countered.

My First Female didn't answer. Her fur spiked along her back. "Just tell them to go!"

"Mitzy," her attention reverted to me. Despite my surprise at finding a wolf in my den, I was curious why they were here. "How long has Lavena been here?"

"In the valley?" At my hiss, she understood. "Oh, you mean here?"

"She boldly dragged her kill inside!" Tomura supplied.

"Lavena wanted to see how Jojo was doing," Mitzy said. "She told me she named him Kayne."

"She tell you why they left him with you?"

Tomura growled again. "It shouldn't matter. Tell the hunter female to take the cub and be gone! Bring some peace to my den. I'm tired of Callie..."

"Enough, Tomura!" I interrupted her. "Go back to your kittens! The wolves are welcome to stay here so I can learn some..."

"Hi, Daddy!" Nan zoomed in with Jojo, or rather Kayne, right behind her.

"Nan! Come back here!" Tomura reached out a paw to try and stop her kitten.

Jojo/Kayne nipped at my first female. She snarled and struck at him. Lavena suddenly stood beside the cub, snarling. Tomura stood her ground. I knew the two would fight if I didn't stop them.

"Stop it!" I placed my large body between the two females. "Tomura, go back to your kittens!" She started to object. "Nan will be fine. Now go!"

With a final glare she haughtily stalked away. The wolf female took a step, but stopped when Mitzy intervened with a gruff sound. Lavena checked the cub, I assumed, to make sure he wasn't hurt. Satisfied, she went back and sat down.

"What are wolves doing here, daddy?" Nan cocked her tiny head looking up at me.

"Seeing how Jojo," no need to confuse her about the rightful name of the cub, "is doing."

"He's fine." Nan trotted over to the female. "He's my littermate."

Inwardly I cringed. Tomura would not like it to find out how close her kitten was to the cub.

Mitzy relayed Nan's comment to Lavena. She lowered her gray head. I noticed the black splotch between her clear blue eyes as she stared at my kitten. Softly she woofed.

"Lavena says she's glad he has a good friend. You're very brave and strong."

"I like Jojo." Nan joined her playmate. Jojo/Kayne had chosen to lie down next to Mitzy's nest. My smallest kitten plopped down between his big paws. He gave her a sloppy lick.

Carefully I came to sit close to my newest mate. "Now, Mitzy, ask her why they left a wolf cub with a feline."

Mitzy asked my question of Lavena. She didn't answer immediately. The two wolves barked between themselves at first, with Jojo adding his voice occasionally. When they stopped the dominate female turned her full attention on us and began to yip, woof, and bark.

My mate listened at first, before beginning to tell me the tale. "The wolves came down into the valley many moonrises ago. It's not that there isn't enough prey. There's plenty of bou and hoppers even if they have to share with the Spotted Ghosts. They," she paused, her ears rotating a bit more forward as Lavena added a few Woofs, "started hearing stories from some of the lone wanderers about the felines in the valley. Particularly one from a male who helped a feline escape a two legged hunter and rescued a kitten."

The wolf who had helped me rescue Sasha! I had always wondered what had become of it. I cleaned a spot on my shoulder quickly, waiting for Mitzy to go on, my excitement growing.

"Lavena decided they should move the pack into the valley and told her daughters what she intended to do. They came as well. Each pack established their own territory, but crossed boundaries sometimes because they're all family."

What all this had to do with Jojo/Kayne ending up with Mitzy I didn't understand. I waited patiently for my question to actually be answered.

"Lavena picked a den, to have her cubs. She chose the big building, the one with all the smashed cars. It was best because it was close to where the grounders burrowed and the pack wouldn't go hungry."

Not far from Dia's stump. No wonder they'd known about her!

"Lavena had her cubs. Jojo, or rather Kayne, was the smallest and she didn't have enough milk to feed him and his stronger siblings."

Choosing the strong over the weak. Our kind did much the same when needed.

"However, she didn't want to starve him. She had the males scout around to see if any felines could take him. They found me. Lavena brought him to me because I was close enough she could still watch over him and provide meat when he got older."

Mitzy had been the closest female I'd claimed. She'd lived in an old store close to the smashed car place and had been quite comfortable living amongst the shabby debris. She'd been rather sad to leave her den.

"When you won me in challenge and we came here, it took her many sunrises to discover where'd we'd gone. Once she did, she provided meat again." Mitzy rumbled quietly. "She's very happy Jojo is with the feline who learned to read. She hoped her cub would learn as well. Seems you are well known, Word Warrior."

I'd never considered the possibility of the wolves hearing about me. In fact, I hadn't even thought about them being intelligent like us. It did begin to explain why they didn't hunt us anymore, as they had in the time of the humans and during the long beginning of winter.

Now another question tugged. "Mitzy, ask her if they know why the long winter came."

My mate inquired. Lavena immediately replied. Mitzy cocked her head, her ears twitching. "She doesn't know. The packs of those days didn't tell the cubs and the knowledge was lost. She's not sure if they even knew."

Even I hadn't found anything in the records at the school. But then, I really hadn't had time to search. My days were spent hunting or instructing the kittens to read while Lara taught the secret of numbers. Though recently, she'd told me Sapphire and Neutron were reading books on Science. They seemed to grasp the principles and theories.

"Tell her thank you. And tell Lavena we've all enjoyed the deer meat. Although where they've managed to find them."

Mitzy blinked. "There are some. The plains beyond us support a small herd, and a well coordinated pack can bring one down."

"Spent time talking about hunting?"

"Of course. As well as how to raise kittens and cubs. Lavena and I have exchanged several secrets and ideas. She likes the fact we all den here together, help raise each other's kittens, and teach our young to hunt. Makes us almost like the hunters."

I really didn't know if I liked the comparison.

~ * ~

Lavena left to rejoin her pack when the sun set. Rowena, for whatever reason, chose to stay. She slept close to Mitzy's nest and as I passed the room with a big rat, I noticed she'd gotten up to check on Dia's kittens. The petite Calico was nursing and washing them and the female seemed fascinated.

I entered the domain of my other mates, dropping their dinner in the middle of the room. Starlite warmly greeted me with a purr, while her two young seriously studied a very large book. I wondered how they'd gotten it in here. Tomura sat on the windowsill while her brood played a rambunctious game of chase and wrestle. Lara's three had joined the game, the group running over the pages, much to the loud objections of Neutron and Sapphire. Lara proceeded to inspect her meal.

"Where's Sasha?" I asked.

"Exploring," Tomura curtly returned. "She said there are a lot of rooms and she didn't know what was in them."

"Waste of time, if you ask me." Callie stood in the door. "Bring me a bit of rat, Lara."

My Maine Coon mate complied dumping a piece before our Elder. Callie sniffed at it, and tore a bite off. Starlite also had some of the rat. Tomura kept sitting on the sill, ignoring my offering.

"Wolf stayed didn't she?" Hatred dripped like blood from the mouth after a kill. Callie's sun yellow eyes blazed, causing her scarred face to make her truly ugly. "Doesn't trust us to care for those kittens."

"Rowena stayed. At least for tonight. I'm sure by sunrise she'll rejoin her pack." I tore off a chunk of meat and jumped up on the sill, laying it before my first female.

"I'm not hungry." She continued to stare out into the darkness.

I jumped down, but left the meat. Taking some for myself, I retreated from my females. Padding down the cold hallway, I entered the room that had once been the school library. I jumped up on a counter and ate my meal.

After my bath, I decided to look around. There were many items everywhere. Some I could identify, others I had no idea. The strangest device had a pale mirror I could vaguely see my reflection on and a piece of plastic with letters and numbers. As I examined it, I couldn't understand why all the letters were mixed up. It made no sense.

Leaping over it, I reached the end and returned to the floor. I investigated many shadowy corners and under bookcases, finding odd treasures. One produced a ball I knew my young would enjoy. Deep under another a bit of string. Yet another had an issue of a magazine, as the humans had once called them.

The front page had been half ripped off. In bold white letters it blared, "President to visit Inuits for…" the rest of the words were gone. I disregarded it and continued searching.

In the back of the library, I found Sasha. She'd found a nice warm spot on top of an old chair and fallen asleep. I leaped up and settled in beside her. I knew I would not be welcome with my females tonight because of the wolves. At least I could keep one of my young warm.

~ * ~

Sharp yips woke me. I opened one eye. Rowena and Jojo/Kayne played together in the middle of the library floor. Nan pranced between their feet determined not to miss any of the fun. Sasha lay beside me, warily watching the canines.

I rose and stretched. Pausing to wash a couple of dirty spots, I had an odd sense of 'rightness'. As if…as if The Provider stroked my fur, reassuring me.

"What lessons are we going to have today?" Sasha asked.

"Many of you are reading well beyond what I can teach," I responded.

"Do you think there are others of our kind who can instruct us in more?"

"I don't know. I had thought I was the only one until Lara came. Perhaps there are others."

"I hope so."

The two wolves had stopped their game, Nan and Jojo choosing to curl up together. Rowena nosed at a fallen book barking at Jojo. The cub answered. She shoved the edition over and he pushed open a page with his nose. His eyes scanned the page and he woofed at her. She studied the page with him.

An odd thought entered my mind. I had seen the cub attend the reading lessons I had given Lara's kittens. Now I knew the wolves were intelligent. Could it be?

Nan gruffly mewed placing her paw on a word. Jojo barked.

"Nan," I left the chair and joined them. "Can Jojo read?"

"Of course, Daddy," she said proudly. "I've been helping him when he doesn't understand."

I knew my smallest daughter was full of surprises. "You did well."

She blinked trusting eyes at me and put her paw on another word.

My stomach rumbled and I knew it was time to hunt again. I moved to leave the room, and jumped several body lengths in the air as a sharp pitched whine filled the library.

Both the wolves howled and Nan and Sasha dashed under the nearest piece of furniture to hide. The sound hurt my ears and I quickly traced the source of my pain. On the high counter the odd mirror flashed bright white. I leapt up and hissed every hair along my back puffing up. With claws extended I tried to stop the awful sound.

The whine abruptly stopped. The mirror faded and all grew quiet again.

"Daddy," Nan called up, "what happened?"

"I don't know." I glared at the source of the noise and jumped down. I had no intention of going near it again.

Sasha slunk out from under the chair we'd slept on. Dodging the wolves she ran out of the room. Nan and Jojo followed. Rowena waited.

"Somehow," I said to her, "I don't think you're going to rejoin your pack."

She barked in response and loped out.

I spared a glance for the thing on the table. What was it and why did it make that noise?

~ * ~

I didn't understand why Starlite chose to move her nest and kittens to another of the rooms. She rearranged the fabric to her satisfaction as Neutron and Sapphire played a game of chase through debris.

"Starlite," I began.

"I've had enough of Tomura's bitterness," she replied before I voiced my question. "She put up with Jojo, but Rowena," she settled down with a sigh, "she doesn't really understand why you permit the hunter female to stay." Her eyes bore into mine. "She seems to be jealous. You do spend a great deal of time with Rowena."

True. I did. The lowest female had a sharp mind and a willingness to learn. I spent the time of sunrise to sunset instructing her.

"Neither you nor Lara, or even Mitzy seem to mind."

"We're not your first female."

"But jealous of a wolf?"

"The two of you had many moonrises together, before I or the others came. She is very fond of you."

Fond of me? I questioned that. She had turned away every choice bit of meat I'd brought her and wouldn't even speak with me.

"Lara's also picked out a room for herself. She feels the same as I. I don't know what you need to do to re-win Tomura, but I suggest, Word Warrior, that you do."

Re-win her, huh? I wondered what I could do to accomplish what seemed an impossible task. I hurried down the dark hallway. I glanced into another room. Lara was resettling her brood.

With resolve, I went to Tomura. My first female lay curled, her back to the door, leaving herself open to attack. Not a wise choice for herself or my kittens, who were not present.

"Tomura," I called from the doorway.

"Go away," she snapped back.

"Where are our kittens?"

"In the library."

"Why are you so bitter?" I couldn't help myself. Tack was not one of my strengths.

"Why!" she nearly screamed. She sprang to her feet, her lean back arched, her chocolate eyes smoldering. "You are such a stupid male!"

"That isn't what you thought when you agreed to my challenge."

"Hunters! You allowed hunters to come here!"

"They haven't harmed our kittens nor hunted us," I reasoned.

She hissed. "Go away!"

Starlite's words came back into my mind. "Are you jealous of Rowena?"

"Of a hunter!" Disdainfully she flicked her tail. "Don't be ridiculous!"

"What then?" I found myself getting tired at her antics.

"Get out!" she ordered again.

"Enough!" I bounded across the room and hit her with my paw.

She staggered back. "How dare you!" She flung herself at me.

We tumbled across the floor, yowling, fighting. Parting we circled, backs arched, hair high along our spines.

"What's all the racket?" Callie grouched from the doorway.

"That's between us!" I snarled back.

"Fighting for domination are we?" Callie huffed. "Never should have allowed a hunter here you know."

"What's done is done. This is my den. You are all my females."

"Is that *all* I am to you?" Tomura threw back.

"What?" Startled, I stopped circling.

"Just a female. Someone to have your kittens. Haven't you learned anything from those books you read?"

"She has a point," Starlite softly spoke. She sat, her fluffy tail curled around her paws. "The humans had something they called love."

Love? I hadn't studied the concept. Males challenged. They won females. Fathered kittens. Provided food.

"You took in a kitten not your own because of human ideas," Starlite reminded me.

"True," I guardedly agreed. "For those same ideals, I allow Jojo and Rowena here."

"But what of us?" Tomura retreated to her nest.

"Might want to think about that great and mighty Word Warrior," Callie taunted, strolling proudly back to her chosen room.

Slinking out of Tomura's place, I passed close to Starlite.

"Much has changed since you first brought us here," she whispered. "We too have learned. We wish to be wives, not just kitten bearers."

"All of you?"

"Why not?" She affectionately licked my muzzle. "You have been better to us than any male ever would have been."

Somehow, I doubted that.

Chapter 8

Wind blew its cold claws though my fur. I shivered but didn't stop. After the events in my den, I decided I needed to go on a long hunt. We had tired of rat and rabbit and even the constant deer Lavena provided us, for the cub and begrudgingly for Rowena. Putting my head down, I pushed forward.

Barking sounded close by. Glancing up, I saw Rowena dashing across the deep mounds. She stopped a body length away and yipped.

"Go back to the school, Rowena. I need to hunt." I trudged on.

She didn't though. The wolf ran out in front, plowing her long nose through the snow like she tracked prey. She looked back at me and waited.

When the sun set, we found shelter in a brick building. Odd machines stood in an open room abandoned by their human keepers. We explored some of the others, finally finding one filled with empty shelves. I wondered what types of books had once filled them.

Rowena woofed and I followed her. We entered a small room. I stopped, stunned. In a corner lay a pile of bones. They looked like they'd been gathered around a container, the sides black as if fire had touched it.

From the pile the wolf pulled a large piece of fabric. She took her prize and found another tiny room to put it. She circled and collapsed on it, looking at me. I crawled beside her, drying my fur and closing my eyes. Her canine warmth joined mine and we slept.

We rose long after the sun began its journey across the clear blue sky. Rowena found a rat and we dined on it before continuing on. More ruined buildings littered the white landscape, many partially buried, others long since collapsed. Skeleton trees stretched their limbs and small tracks in the snow reminded us of the other creatures who shared our world.

We found other tracks too. Odd long ones, with regular deep gouges. Nor were they covered by the frequent storms, like the last ones I had tried to follow.

I started looking around for places to hide. If the metal monster had made these, I wanted a place we could retreat to quickly. Even Rowena didn't range as far ahead. She kept close, whining occasionally, peering uneasily at the path I had chosen.

Snow began to fall. Despite my discomfort at getting wet, I was thankful. The storm would make it more difficult for us to be seen. We could more easily sneak up on whatever creatures inhabited the machine. I knew also, we could lose the trail.

Could it be humans? And so, were they hunters? Would we be their prey? We felines carried no memories of them, other than the stories our elders told. Or in my case I could include the pictures I'd seen in books.

The snow lessened and the sun arched across the sky. It sat on the mountains as it took the light with it. Rowena and I traveled on, following the scored snow. We came to a place of more smashed cars and the building they had once surrounded, now nothing but tumbled brick and snapped wood.

The path veered and headed for the mountains. I stopped, my bushy tail slowly waving as I considered. Did we dare keep following? Would it truly be wise?

Rowena woofed. I sensed she was waiting for me to make a decision. If humans had truly returned to our world, perhaps, just perhaps, it might be wise to discover the truth and see if I could uncover what they might be searching for.

As we trotted on, full dark fell upon us. My eyes adjusted and I took the lead with Rowena behind me. No moon shined down. Clouds heavy with snow dumped their weight. I knew we should find shelter for the night. We crossed under an old overpass and I vaguely saw a half - crumpled building.

Leaving the path we followed, we struggled in the high drifts and finally found shelter. The many windows were broken, the door busted completely. We entered a room with a long counter. Cold blasts shook and howled wolf like through the room.

Rowena dashed through and down a long hallway. I ran after her. In a cramped room she took cover, whining and shivering. It offered some protection from the wind and I noticed the washer and dryer and other odd things hanging on the walls.

Quickly I dried myself with my tongue. The female went out to shake the water from her fur. She disappeared briefly and reappeared dragging something large, pulling it into our sleeping spot. Bunching it up, she finally laid down. I joined her.

Wind rushed down the hall. Our chosen sleeping spot was not as warm as the night before. I burrowed under the heavy fabric like a rabbit in its hole and finally fell into an exhausted sleep.

Rumbling noise and the floor shaking woke us. I panicked not remembering how I came to be so entangled. Finally I freed myself. Rowena stood by the door, a low growl in her throat. Slinking along the cold, snowy floor, I joined her.

Together we crept down the hall into the broken window room. We approached the open door cautiously looking out. The metal monster I had seen long ago when it passed my den staggered past, one long leg lurching as if it were injured.

It stopped. My ears went back and I hissed. Rowena growled. Openings appeared in the side. Two legged creatures emerged. They gathered around the hurt limb. One lifted an appendage sort of like the arms I'd read about and pointed toward our hiding spot.

Without thought we ran. We leaped over busted beams and found an open door and a broken window. Racing over the edge we both rolled in the drift. Rowena yipped pulling herself free. I floundered, not able to get a foothold.

Canine teeth grabbed my neck and pulled. Rowena set me down and we heard harsh sounds. We turned facing the two-legged invaders. I recognized the large net they carried, having seen smaller ones carried by similar hunters. Darting under a skeleton tree, I escaped. Rowena snarled.

I looked back. They'd almost caught her. She'd jumped aside just in time and now their net was entangled in the tree. I ran ahead hoping Rowena would follow.

A crackling sound split the air. Rowena whined but kept running. We raced across the snow, fear pumping our every step. Finally, when I could no longer breathe, I allowed myself to slow down. My heart pounded.

Rowena wobbly stood beside me, her blue eyes glassy, foam dripping from her mouth. Frantically I searched for a place we could hide and rest. An old house, half buried, wasn't very far away.

I rubbed against Rowena encouraging her. She staggered but managed. Once inside she fell to the ripped carpeted floor. The Provider at least had been kind. We were far enough in to be protected from the wind. Her body lay still. I sniffed along her fur trying to find where she'd been hurt.

Finding no wound I was puzzled. All I found was an odd tube with red fringe on top embedded in her hindquarters. I grabbed it with my teeth and tugged until it came loose. It rolled to the floor. The end I couldn't see had a long sharp nose.

Scuttling sounds. Rats. Good. I hunted one and had a good meal, catching another for Rowena. I placed it on the floor close by. She'd see it when she woke up. Or at least I hoped she'd wake up.

The house shook and lightning parted the falling flakes. I jumped up on a tattered couch near a window. The snow fell heavily. Rowena and I might be here for awhile. More zagged light. I blinked but used the advantage to search for the two-legged invaders. There seemed to be none.

Relieved, I returned to Rowena. At least we'd be safe. I bathed myself and lay down next to her my side against her back. I needed to keep her warm. Putting my large head down on my front paws, I faced the door, alert to any movement or sound. During the time just before the sun rose, I heard the stuttering cry of the metal monster.

Rowena stirred beside me weakly. She whined. I got up and tried to reassure her by licking her long nose. Also, I hoped to quiet her. The snow had covered our tracks and I doubted the humans, if humans they were, would be able to find us.

Odd crunching noises reached my ears. A low screech and I hid behind Rowena, my body crouched low and I hoped, out of sight. There was no way to hide her and I regretted that.

"Word Warrior," another male called. I could smell his strong scent.

I carefully glanced around. He stood just inside a doorway leading deeper inside the old house. His coloring I had never seen. He had long sandy colored fur with gray stripes. He blinked blue eyes.

"I'll distract them while you try and get that hunter on its feet." He dashed through the front door.

Loud shrill calls bounced outside. I leaped over Rowena and began urging her up. It took several attempts before she stood and I gently nudged her toward the door where the other male had been. She almost fell, but I kept forcing her on, not knowing how long the strange male could keep the two legged invaders away.

Rowena lurched into what had to once have been a kitchen and I found the back door open. We floundered outside and headed across the expanse. I had to constantly keep watch on my companion as she could only take a few steps, then had to rest.

I saw a metal tunnel large enough for her to enter and headed for it. Rowena slowly seemed to get stronger and better able to keep going. I thanked The Provider and ran. We reached the tunnel and hurried inside. The dank stench hurt my nose. Grit and mold littered the bottom. I paused, allowing Rowena a rest.

"Good choice." The male who had aided us earlier observed. He stepped closer so I could clearly see him. "The two legs, humans aren't they? Are now chasing some grazers. They lost interest in me."

"Thank you for helping us," I replied. "And I think perhaps they're humans."

"You won my sister." He cleaned ice from between his toes.

"And which of my females is your sister?"

"Starlite. I'm her brother, Algier."

~ * ~

She dragged in the horned one she'd been fortunate enough to kill. Her three cubs bounded over, tearing off meat and swiping at each other for the best parts. Anumati took some as well, dropping a small piece in front of Snow Fur. Her foundling sniffed at it and nibbled on the meat.

Truthfully, she hadn't been certain if he was old enough for meat yet. She'd probably have to give him some milk later. She settled down on the pine boughs and ate.

Her cubs finished their meal and tumbled around with each other. The play fighting they were doing would serve them well as they grew older. She glanced over at the small white feline as he finished eating and washed himself. He got up and wandered off into the back of the cave.

Anumati had noticed Snow Fur spent much of the day there and would return as dark fell to sleep with her and her cubs. Vaguely she wondered what he found to do, but didn't really worry about him. At least he didn't run the risk of getting squashed by her rambunctious three.

She put her head down on her paws. After the long hunt, her belly now full, she'd earned a nap. She closed her eyes and rested, listening to playful snarls. When she opened her eyes again, Snow Fur had returned. Somehow he'd dragged an odd feathery thing with him.

Intently he gazed at her and put his paw down causing a faint scratchy noise. Slowly she dropped her eyelids not understanding. Again he deliberately lifted his tiny paw and put it down again.

She got up and stood behind him. Strange markings reminding her of tree bark were on the thing he'd found. "I don't understand," she told him.

Snow Fur ran across the cave to the entrance, jumped out and back in, jumped out again and then inside, running back to put his paw on one of the marks. She noticed the markings separated between themselves. Studying them she began to get curious about what they were and where her foundling had discovered them.

"I still don't understand," she sadly told him.

~ * ~

We traveled the tunnel while the sun sat behind heavy clouds dropping more snow. No doubt we'd journey in the storm if we weren't sheltered as the flakes fell. Algier lead as he knew these ways. Finally we emerged into the dim light and the falling wet.

"There's a place we can stay," he informed us.

He bounced through the drifts until he reached a rounded brick building. High piles of snow covered one side and part of the ceiling had caved in. He darted in a large crack and I followed. Rowena managed to squeeze through.

As my eyes adjusted to the dim light, I stood amazed. Shelves upon shelves of books surrounded the huge room. I couldn't believe it!

"One of the old libraries," Algier commented.

"Are there more of these?"

"Many. Including one close to your den."

I wondered why I hadn't discovered it for myself. I thought I had explored most of the buildings in my territory.

"You have." He trotted over to one of the shelves. "You wouldn't notice it because it's trapped in the ice."

Now I knew which building he meant! I would have to explore it again to see if there was a way in. "Thank you," I replied, suddenly realizing he'd answered a question I hadn't voiced.

"Gift from my mother. My sister 'sees' future events. I read the minds of others."

"Just who was your mother?" I sat down, resting my tail over my paws warming them.

"I don't know."

Rowena barked. I had temporarily forgotten her.

"She's hungry," Algier informed me.

"Any rats close by?"

He was silent as if my question made no sense. "Not here," he finally replied. "But there is a field where the grounders live. Prairie dogs I think the humans called them."

"Do you know how to read, Algier?"

"Yes. And I have a very good grasp of Science and Physics."

"Starlite's kittens would love to have you teach them. Neither I nor Lara really understand the concepts."

"You would have me join you? Another male?" His surprise I understood. Males never shared dens.

"As long as you don't challenge me for my females."

"They think too much. Hurts my head. That's why I've never challenged for any."

He never had? Not sure what to make of that revelation I asked, "Would living in my den be too difficult?"

Algier sneezed. "At least your females probably think about more than mating, kittens and hunting. Sounds like you have at least one who also instructs."

"I do. But I don't know what my females do think about. And I have many kittens. Including those not my own. There are better ways." I waited for his reaction.

"I agree," Algier paused. "I'll go hunt. You and Rowena explore the library. Maybe you can find information that will help us survive better."

"Maybe." Not really understanding why that might be important.

The other male left. I glanced up at Rowena. "Shall we explore?" She yipped in response as if she understood and knocked some books onto the floor.

Algier returned much later with scrawny catches. We ate the meat and spent much of the dark climbing shelves, dropping books down, and searching their pages. Even Rowena stuck her long nose into the books. I knew I had instructed her, so she must be reading.

"She is." Algier stopped beside me. "She learned along with the cub. Seems your little kitten is a good teacher as are you."

"Nan considers Jojo her littermate."

Rowena's excited yelps summoned us. We both dashed to her side. The wolf shoved the book over to us and we both studied the words.

"The Great," I read. Some of the words were gone. "When the warnings of the astronomers first began to be listened to…evidence began to show…"

"What evidence?" Algier wanted to know.

"I don't know. Sometimes, I wish we had a more complete history. There seem to be things not written."

"Like how this world became like it is."

"We may never learn that," I told him.

"What else does it say?" Algier's tail slowly swished.

I glanced at the page before me. "This event did not in and of itself begin The Great... World wide poverty levels plus overcrowding with vague promises of better more prosperous lives, began the slow rush to... About a quarter of the population had relocated when astronomers intensified their warnings...."

"Well?"

I tried to turn the page. Many instead of just one turned. The words now talked about something called protein bars. Gently I used my claws to try and separate the pages. I couldn't. Sometime during this long winter the pages had stuck together.

Algier noticed too. "Guess we won't find out today."

Disappointed I pushed the book aside. What had begun as a promising find now tasted of bitter, stale meat. Perhaps we would never learn what had happened to our world.

"At least we know there are some records. Maybe we'll be fortunate and find more," Algier said.

I could only hope the Provider would so indulge us. "We should rest and then head for my den."

~ * ~

Anumati led her cubs back into their snug den. They pranced around each other bragging, sending praises and thanks to Sekhmet for her generosity. She watched and listened with pride. They'd brought down their first horned one, given the due blood offering to the fierce goddess and eaten their fill.

Snow Fur didn't glance up. He was again entranced in whatever those strange markings were. Kerani pranced over the brittle stuff. He swiped at her. She snarled and rejoined her siblings in the victory celebration.

"Snow Fur," Anumati addressed him.

The bundle of white fur ignored her. Irritated she butted him with her head sending him tumbling head over tail. He peered at her with surprised blue eyes.

"Soon it will be your turn to hunt."

He cocked his head and blinked. Walking back to his markings, he glanced at her, and returned his attention to his task.

Unsure of what to do next or how to get him to be involved in her family's joy, she decided to leave him and joined her cubs in a game of play fighting.

~ * ~

We left the library as the sun set over the white covered mountains. I didn't like the idea of traveling during the dark, but we'd heard that strange metal monster again and decided to use the blackness as cover to escape the notice of the two-legged invaders.

A sliver of moon graced the black sky companioned by a bright twinkling star. I paused to admire the pair. Rowena ran on ahead and Algier stopped to gaze up as well.

"The star is the planet Venus," he informed me.

"I'd read our system has ten planets."

"And an asteroid belt." He jumped suddenly to the side chasing after a small squeaker.

I joined him in the game and pursued the creature until it escaped through a small crack in the ice. We continued on staying silent through the cold crisp wilderness. We stopped when the sun first crested on the distant plains.

Taking refuge in a store, we hunted rats and settled down for a meal of rodent. I washed my fur clean, as did Algier while Rowena roamed the store, poking her nose under fabrics and debris, her tail constantly wagging.

She brought back a long length of soft stuff for us to sleep on. The three of us curled up together for warmth, but sleep didn't come immediately. My thoughts were back in the library and trying to figure out how to transport the wonderful books full of more knowledge back to my den's library.

"We need some way to transport them," I murmured.

"The humans, back in the past, constructed wagons," Algier suggested.

"How would we do that?" Intelligent though I was, I didn't have any way to build anything.

"In some of the houses I've been in there have been small wagons. I think their young played with them. We could search for some."

"But how do we get the wagons and then the books into them?"

"The hunters, wolves are strong enough."

Of course! The wolves! Well, maybe just Rowena and Jojo. I doubted any of the others would help.

"Wouldn't hurt to ask." Algier closed his eyes. "Now stop thinking and go to sleep so I can."

I laid my head on my paws trying to relax and sleep. Too many delightful ideas kept coming into my mind and I wanted to run and accomplish the task. Now!

Rowena rubbed her head on my back. Licking her nose, I allowed myself to relax and sleep.

~ * ~

We dined on rat again before continuing on. A storm had blown in and we pressed against the fierce wind and the blinding snow. We traveled close together to help each other so we wouldn't become lost.

Snow melted on my fur and dripped down to my skin. Chill set in even as I pressed on. I had explored this area before and knew we could reach the den by sunrise. When we finally climbed the hill to the school, we tumbled in, Rowena shaking herself and Algier and myself drying our wet fur.

"Daddy!" Nan bounded over, Jojo behind her.

The two wolves greeted each other with licks, rubs and howling. My kittens surrounded me and each babbled a story while we walked the dark hallways to the library. The females all looked up from the book they were reading. Callie was absent.

"Knew it had gotten too quiet," Mitzy fondly said.

"And who is this!" Tomura demanded her sleek fur ruffled.

"Algier!" Starlite cried happily. She bounced over to her brother and the two touched noses. "It has been so long!"

"Yes, it has, sister," he tiredly replied. "I'd heard who won you in challenge."

"How did you meet Word Warrior?"

My kittens scurried around all wanting to hear the story. Tomura huffed, but waited patiently while we told our tale.

"So you know Science and Physics," Lara remarked when we finished. "It will be good for Neutron and Sapphire to have someone who can teach them."

"And it seems Blythe also has an interest in science as well," Mitzy added.

I'd almost forgotten about the other two kittens I'd rescued. "What about the other?"

"Ellen likes As..tron..omy." My mate struggled with the word.

"One who likes the stars. Good." Algier sat. "When the time of dark comes again, and if there is no storm, we'll go out and study the constellations."

"Goody!" my kittens all yelled.

Sasha touched my nose and I noticed Algier's immediate interest. I wondered if he might challenge me for her when she came into her first heat.

"Tomura intends her for Word Warrior," I heard Starlite tell her brother.

He blinked. "We'll see."

Chapter 9

Algier and I searched around the school to find a room for him. He didn't want to be close to the females and kittens because all their thinking made his head hurt. We followed a short hall and took frosted stairs down into a large room with a slick brown floor.

"I can't hear them here." Algier gingerly crossed the floor.

Exploring the room we discovered odd folding stairs along the concrete walls, a stage, I think the humans called it, and heavy, ripped blue curtains sagged from the ceiling. Part of the dusty fabric spread across the platform.

"I'll come to the library to teach the kittens," he said as he made himself comfortable in the folds. "When I'm not there I'll be in here or hunting."

I sat. I had a question I needed to ask him. "Will you help me defend my females and kittens?" At the previous sunset I'd sniffed around the school. Midnight had been by and left his scent for me to find. I sensed he would soon challenge me.

"If it comes to it," Algier agreed. "I have no desire for my sister to end up with another male, particularly Midnight."

"Good." I rose and left.

Rowena met me end of the hallway and together we returned to the library. Nan and Jojo sprawled on the tattered carpet, reading a book. Lara instructed others in Math, and Mitzy zagged about overseeing the rest as they played games of chase.

Tomura rested on a chair, her thin regal tail hanging over the edge. I jumped up to join her. She licked my nose and we lay together in contented silence.

Starlite came in greeting Rowena, Nan, and Jojo before gathering her two kittens from the game. "Neutron, Sapphire, it's time to hunt rat."

"Ah, Mom," Neutron groaned.

"Hunting is important to learn and practice. How else are you going to eat?"

The three left and Lara's Math lesson ended. Freed, her students joined the game as their mothers watched nearby.

"I'm glad you're home, Word Warrior," Tomura softly greeted me.

"You're not angry about the wolves anymore." At least I hoped she wasn't.

"It wasn't just about the wooolves." She elongated the unfamiliar word.

"All of you want to be wives."

"That, and I'm your first mate. I felt like you should have talked to me first before allowing wolves here."

"And I'm the male. This is my den."

"We are changing husband. The more we learn of the humans, the more some of their ideas appeal to us."

"Like being wives and not just females."

"Exactly. You taught us to read. You taught us to take in kittens not our own. You've even taught us to accept the wolves, albeit reluctantly." Briefly her eyes rested on Nan and Jojo.

I knew where her thoughts were going and I didn't even share Algier's ability. "So I must change as you, my females have."

"Is it such an unpleasant idea?" Her chocolate eyes met mine.

"It will take time." The idea made me slightly uneasy.

"All things do."

~ * ~

Snow Fur limped back into the den. Anumati followed with the dead large foot, which was to have been his first kill, hanging in her mouth. She dropped her prey, her cubs watching uneasily as her foundling settled on his warm furs.

When the sun had risen she'd taken her foundling on his first hunt. He'd struggled in the deep drifts and she'd finally had to stop and leave him in one spot. She'd searched for a large foot and chased it in the direction she wished.

Snow Fur had floundered after it, constantly falling. She'd yowled to freeze their intended prey. The animal had froze, its sides heaving, nose twitching.

The smaller feline had stopped as well, not knowing what to do. He'd looked up at her and back to the large foot.

A suspicion had formed in her mind. She'd yowled again. Snow Fur hadn't reacted She'd growled. Still no reaction. Sadly, she'd pounced on the large foot, snapped its neck and returned to the den with their prey.

"I'm taking the large foot to Sanjiv," she told her cubs.

"Then what will we eat?" Jyotis demanded.

"You're old enough to catch your own meal." She took the dead carcass in her mouth and set off across the snow. When she reached the old one's den she entered and offered it to him.

Slowly he raised his head sniffing her offering. "You've asked nothing of me recently."

"You were right about Snow Fur," she confessed. "I should take him back to the valley. To the feline who can read."

"What has happened for this revelation?" He licked his paw.

"I took him on his first hunt."

He waited in silence. She knew he sensed there was more.

"And he cannot hear."

~ * ~

I explored the area where Algier had told me another library stood. Rowena joined me, as did Jojo and Nan. My tiny kitten rode on Jojo's back, her yowls of delight echoing in the crisp air.

"Stay here," I ordered. Slipping through a crack in the ice I carefully followed the winding track trying not to slip and hoped I didn't get stuck. Under the thick layers I found bent frames and broken glass. Complete darkness met my eyes. I waited and vague shadows took form.

A long desk with odd things on it, carpeted floor now covered with broken furniture, high shelves, many of them bare, but others with a few precious books on them. Exploring further, I found corners with stacked piles of magazines, some newspapers in another small room, and bones huddled under a table.

Following the same path out, I rejoined my daughter and the wolves.

"What did cha' find, Daddy?"

"Books. Nan, would you ask Rowena if she knows of any other wolves who would help us take these books from here and transport them back to our den?"

I waited while she asked. Algier had gone on a scouting mission and managed to find a couple of wagons. Rowena had gone with him to bring back his finds.

"Rowena says two of her brothers might. She'll go ask them."

The female dashed off. I walked back to our den with Jojo and Nan.

There was no way to tell how long it might take Rowena to find her pack and return.

Nan slid off Jojo's back and joined the rest of my kittens around Callie. Our Elder sat on the chair in the library, her orange body draped easily on the edge.

"Nice you could join us, Nan," she said. Her tail flipped in agitation as Jojo took his place beside his friend.

I knew she'd never actually accepted Jojo nor Rowena. She just seemed to resign herself to the fact they were here and there was nothing she could do about it.

"Tonight my dears, I will tell you a story my Elder told me."

~ * ~

She would miss her cozy den. Anumati stood poised at the entrance, Snow Fur on her back and her cubs grumbling beside her. She knew it was best to take her foundling to the valley and leave it with others like himself.

Yet, a part of her did not want to give up her small foundling. Still, she understood he would eventually die because he could not hunt and could not hear, a deadly combination in the stormy high mountains where she lived.

"Why do we have to leave, Mom?" Jyotis wanted to know.

"Snow Fur needs to go back to the valley."

"You could just take him and we could stay here," Kerani suggested.

"You're too young to be left alone yet. I still have much to teach you."

"I think we should listen to, Mom." Valmiki excitedly twitched his tail. "Just think of it sisters! We're going on an adventure!"

"An adventure he says," Kerani complained as she followed her mother.

The sun sat high on the mountains as they slowly traversed the trail heading down. Pines laden heavy with snow bent over the iced streams. Large foot and horned ones tracks mixed liberally beside it, showing where they had drunk during the night.

"Can we go hunting, mom?" Jyotis looked hopefully up at her.

"Not until we den during the dark. We'll hunt then."

Her daughter growled quietly, but didn't argue. Valmiki bounded through the drifts totally enjoying himself. Kerani trailed slowly behind.

Valmiki dashed past his mother and playfully swatted at his sister.

Kerani snarled and the two took off chasing each other. Jyotis stayed beside Anumati.

"How long will it take us?" Jyotis brushed against her mother's shoulder.

"Many suns and moons," she answered.

The path narrowed and she noted with approval Jyotis automatically dropped behind her. Anumati glided past jutting rock and finally spotted her two other cubs. They'd stopped in the small valley below and were investigating the area. She hurried down, being careful not to dump Snow Fur, who still rode on her back.

"What's this interesting smell, Mom?" Valmiki wanted to know.

Anumati sniffed the track and part of the surrounding area, drawing back with a hiss, her heart beating fast. Frantically she scanned the area for any threat. "It would not be good for us to stay here. When the large white swiper returns, it might decide we're prey."

"What's a swiper?" Valmiki fell into a trot beside her as she led her cubs away from possible danger.

"After the storms came, they came. They hunt the horned ones and large foot."

"Where'd they come from?"

"From a land that has always been snow."

"And where's that?"

"Far away."

~ * ~

We all stood around the ice crack which, lead down into the library. As she'd promised Rowena had returned with two of her brothers. The males had taken what looked like rope into their mouths and pulled the odd wagons with metal runners on them here. Algier had gone down below and I could hear him muttering as he dragged up the first book, it's cover in his teeth.

He cleared the entrance. Rowena waited until he relenquished it before she took in her mouth and dropped the new source of knowledge onto a wagon. I slipped past the other male and took my turn bringing up a book.

We continued to load the wagons until the sun began to touch the mountains. Then each of the wolves again grabbed the ropes and started back to the school. The going was slower, as the wagons were much heavier, and we were going uphill.

A couple of books dropped off and Rowena acted as rear-guard snatching each out of the snow and returning it to its proper place. The sun had fallen to its far resting place when we finally reached my den.

The wolves helped unload and the three loped off. I'd had them put the new books in a corner of the library. Later, I'd go through them to see what knowledge we'd recovered.

"I'm going to find me a nice fat juicy rat and eat," Algier told me as he left us.

"Why didn't you let me go with you, daddy?" Nan complained. My smallest kitten sat on the shredded rug, her yellow eyes holding a hurt look.

"As I said before we left, I didn't want you to get hurt."

"You just didn't want me to get in the way."

Partially true. I also didn't know if I could trust the two male wolves with one of my young.

Jojo stuck his long nose in the pile of books. He barked excitedly.

"What did ya find?" Nan ran to him.

He grabbed one thick volume and dumped it open. He pushed pages aside with his nose and stopped, his tail wagging.

I wandered over to see what new discovery the cub had made. The book seemed to be one filled with pictures. Laying before me was a gentle meadow with a crooked stream meandering through it. Tall pines lined the far edge and a human stood in the middle of the water holding a long stick. I had no idea what the creature was doing.

Nan cocked her head listening to Jojo's barks. "He says the wolves came from here. They've been away for a long time and then came back. They started traveling and making more territories for themselves."

"And where is there?" I waited while she translated.

"He doesn't really know. He said it is far away."

Rowena had to be telling him some of the wolf's history. I'd heard the two of them howling together or sometimes just quietly yipping.

"A place far away," Tomura mused as she joined us. She gave me a friendly nuzzle. She glanced at the picture. "Looks green and wonderful."

"It was a long time ago. When the humans were here," Nan told her.

Jojo turned another page. More odd pictures, one side showed a building made of logs and another had some sort of strange white mound. It reminded me of a mound of snow, but since not all the ground wasn't covered that couldn't be what it was.

I tried to read the words underneath. They didn't make sense, although they did seem to be scientific. Later, I'd ask Algier to look at them. Maybe he could tell me what a geyser was.

~ * ~

When the sun set they stopped in a hollow underneath a fallen log. Her cubs joined her while she hunted for a large foot. She successfully caught one, her young did not. When they returned to their temporary shelter she dropped their meal on the snowy dirty ground tearing off a small piece for Snow Fur.

Her foundling huddled in a corner, tightly curled, trying to keep warm. She left him some food and took her share of the kill. After her nightly wash, she curled up, her cubs beside her and Snow Fur resting between her paws.

Wind rushed through the thick pines. She'd noticed how many more there were further down. Many more than the high peaks where she lived. Misty cold drifted in and she was glad they could huddle together and share their body's warmth.

Anumati dozed lightly, keeping alert for any sound of danger. She did not want to be surprised by a swiper. In her young days, her mother had been inattentive and had lost her only brother to one of the massive hungry beasts. She had no intention of repeating that mistake.

When the sun rose, the small party continued downward. The snow glistened under the bright sunbeams. Anumati found herself hoping the good weather continued and no storms would strike on their journey. Perhaps Sekhmet would be kind and favor them.

~ * ~

We'd spent much of the time from sunset to sunrise searching the new books for knowledge. My kittens had all been excited, batting at each other, playing games of chase and pushing each other aside to read what the pages had to say.

When the sun had risen, their mothers had finally rounded their young up and sent them off to various nests to sleep. Jojo and Nan had slept in the library. So had I, on the chair, where I could watch the two of them and the door, in case the other wolves returned.

Rattling jarring noises woke us. I jumped over to the windowsill. Two legged creatures crawled out of a large metal rectangular monster, gesturing with their upper limbs. Jojo growled below me.

"Tell him to be quiet, Nan," I ordered.

The two legs came toward the window. I hunched down, not moving. Round dark eyes peered inside and I heard strange noises. They moved away. I waited briefly and leaped down. "Nan, go find a place for you and Jojo to hide."

They scurried away and out the far door. I ran down the hall, poking my head in various rooms and telling my females and kittens to hide. Starlite and her two dashed into Callie's abode. I knew they'd warn our Elder.

Finding a broken beam to hide under, I hunkered down and waited. Crunching reached my ears. Three shadows fell into the hallway near the main door. Two were huge and the third much smaller. They were covered in bright orange with odd clear things over a space near the top of them. I did not know their smell.

The two huge ones walked in, but the smaller hesitated. More odd noises, one deep, the other higher. I could only surmise it was some type of communication. They went down the hallway. I stayed where I was, too afraid to move and risk being seen.

Loud sounds echoed down the hall in changing pitches. Part of me wanted to go see what they were doing in our library, yet the other terrified part kept me still. After a long while the three went past me and back out into the bright sunshine. The monster shuddered awake and droned away.

I went from room to room checking on my females and kittens. They were all safe. I returned to the library to see if the two-legs had taken anything.

"They looked at the thing up there," Nan told me as I jumped up on the counter.

Their strange scent covered everything. The odd box mirror, the keys with the out of order letters and numbers, other objects they'd touched.

"What made this so interesting?" I wondered aloud.

"The two legs didn't seem to notice all the books," Nan went on.

"That's good." At least our learning was safe.

Jojo woofed and followed the two-legs' trail out. Nan bounced after him. If any of the two legs came back again, the wolf would recognize them, as would I. I comforted myself with the thought while yet another came to me. What would we do if they came back and discovered us? Might I have to come up with a plan to defend my den from the unknown two-legged intruders?

Chapter 10

Two full moons later Anumati and her cubs found old human dwellings. Several log structures, bent and busted, littered the lower hillside. A large frozen lake extended down the narrow valley with a small brick building sitting beside it.

"Where should we sleep tonight, Mother?" Kerani gingerly tested the frozen over surface.

The brick building looked intact and would probably be much safer than any of the log structures. "There."

She started across the lake, completely confident the ice would support her weight. Her cubs followed each unsure at first and then relaxing as nothing happened. Climbing the slight embankment she walked around the building to the front. Maybe once the entrances had been covered, but now only dark holes stared out at them.

Anumati crouched down and allowed Snow Fur to jump down off her back. Cautiously she investigated the structure. The floor was snow covered and smelled strongly of red tail. One must have denned here recently. Some sort of container sat mounted on the wall and odd round others sat on the floor.

She stretched her lithe body, placing her paws on the wall container. Another of her kind stared back at her. She snarled a challenge. The stranger didn't respond. She blinked her eyes. So did the other. Putting her paw against it, instead of feeling warm fur, all she felt was a cold hard surface. Deciding it was not a threat, she got down and summoned her cubs inside.

"It stinks," Kerani compained.

"But this place will shelter us for the night. Where's Snow Fur?"

"I'll get him," Valmiki volunteered, reappearing with her foundling. "He was just outside."

The cubs wrestled while she further searched the shelter. Snow Fur jumped up on the container and amused himself with the odd shiny surface above it.

"What are we going to sleep on?" Jyotis wanted to know.

"I'll go see what I can find. All of you stay here." She went back outside.

A cold breeze ruffled her fur and tangy storm scent reached her nose. They might be here for several sunrises. She didn't really want to travel during snow and risk losing any of her precious cubs.

Racing back across the frozen lake she darted through a crack in one of the log buildings. She explored the interior finding something that looked like a fur, yet the smell told her it wasn't any type of prey she knew. Dragging it back, she got it through the drifts and back into their shelter.

Her cubs inspected her find and went back to playing. When dark fell they all curled up together. Wind ripped though the valley shaking the overhead covering. Anumati rested her head on her paws, listening to the sound. Her now night adjusted eyes watched large flakes fall.

Her plan had been to follow the lake down the valley. Now, she'd have to wait out the storm before they could continue. They still had more distance to travel. Findingthese dwellings buoyed her tired body and spirit.

She hoped soon they'd find the large valley and could then begin her important search of finding the feline who could read. She'd be sad to lose Snow Fur. She cared for him as if he were one of her own cubs.

Snow began to pile up at the entrance. Normally this would concern her. However, the barrier it would form would give them more protection from the cold and storm. She sent a silent thank you to Sekhmet for her gracious gift of a shelter and would have to remember to give the goddess a blood offering with her next kill.

A faint scratching sound outside made her heart beat faster. She'd never heard of swipers this low in the mountains. She watched as a long nose intruded into their shelter and a growl escaped her throat.

A shaggy howler head popped up in surprise and cocked it to one side. Woofing deeply the howler carefully moved its massive body to the far side. Slowly it sank down lying on the cold slick floor.

Startled by its unusual behavior, she made no aggressive move, waiting to see what the unexpected intruder would do next. It shivered and shifted trying to get warm. Snow Fur crawled from his spot beside her paw and approached the howler while she wasn't looking. Anumati turned her head in time to watch the exchange, not exactly sure what was going on. Her protective instincts took over and she tensed flexing her claws ready to pounce. The howler moved its nose close to Snow Fur. The tongue darted out and she readied for an attack. The howler merely licked her adoptive cub on his face in what seemed to her a friendly gesture, since the intruder made no move to snap Snow Fur's neck. Her foundling strolled back, circled a couple of times, and lay back beside her paw. Nervously she glanced at the howler, still not certain what it wanted.

The howler barked, the tone almost inquiring. What was it asking she wondered? It rose, hesitantly approaching her. Again a tremor shook its body. She made no move and waited. Her once possible aggressor laid down close by, just on edge of the odd fur, closed its eyes and went to sleep.

Then she understood. It wanted to be on something warm and not on the cold floor. That had been its way of asking permission to be on the fur. By making no threatening movements herself, the howler had taken Anumati's lack of response as permission. And since it had acted so friendly with Snow Fur, maybe this was its way of saying it was no threat to her or her cubs? Or maybe the howler knew others of her kind. But how could that be?

Her mind full of these musings she stayed awake long into dark, listening to the rattling shelter and still uneasy about the howler's intentions.

When the sun rose she knew from looking outside, they would not be traveling. Snow fell so thickly she couldn't even see the edge of the mountain she knew was close by. The howler still slept and her cubs played cautiously, snarling at each other when their sibling was not where they'd expected them to be.

Her foundling was again up on the container, patting at the shiny image. He jumped back down just as the howler opened its eyes. It wagged its tail and yipped in what sounded like a greeting.

"He can't hear you," Anumati said. Clear blue eyes stared at her. "Not…hear…"

Blinking her own in surprise she stood watching the howler. Surely she hadn't heard, what she thought she'd just heard!

"Cat…not…hear…."

"You, understand me?"

"Some."

She didn't know what to make of this development. No howler had ever been able to understand her. At least now she knew her suspicion they'd crossed over to intelligence was justified.

"How?" Her curiosity roused, she again settled on the fur thing. "Long…tell…."

"The storm isn't going to stop soon."

"I…Dermot…lowly male…."

Anumati listened as his story unfolded. Her mind attempted to supply missing details as his ability to grasp her tongue proved difficult. Wind rattled the metal roof and she soon forgot about that, and his inability to fully communicate correctly…

˷ * ˷

Dermot played at the edge of the pack with one of his brothers. The mating ritual between the dominant pair was about to begin and his attendance was expected. He and his sibling stopped the wrestling game rejoining the pack around their leaders.

Brenna, the female, had just come into heat, yet Dermot had seen her and Eoin, their pack leader, constantly together during the last several sunrises. He'd seen many matings in his lifetime, so the affection shown between the two was not something new. Besides, this was an exciting time for the pack as puppies would be added and their family would increase.

Eoin proceeded with the mating and the two continued the behavior for several full suns. Finally, Brenna began to search for and dig a den to birth her pups. Instead of the den under the dead logs she'd used before, she chose a new spot higher in the mountains under the roots of white dead trees. Dermot joined the others hunting, and bringing back pieces of meat, burying the choice bits in the soft earth, for the dominate female to eat later while she cared for the new pups.

Just before the sun rose he left the pack on yet another hunt. Dermot jumped across the frozen stream and climbed the steep bank searching for bit track. He'd seen several of the tasty creatures just as the sun set. He'd dreamed of them and had decided when he woke they would be a welcome change to the mainly bou diet. He hoped Brenna would agree and reward him a chance for approval.

The cold wind had frozen the snow making his progress easy. His large feet didn't sink. He was used to traveling the land of white. He yipped in happiness and ran further up the mountain. Dermot loved to run free apart from the pack and away from the constant torment of his brothers and sisters.

He stopped. Huge embedded tracks caught his attention. The ambler's were fierce predators and could be a threat to the pack and future pups. He investigated and much to his relief the trail moved away from the new den and not towards it. He'd heard stories of the lumbering creatures eating just born pups. If it had been traveled anywhere near them, he would have immediately returned and warned the pack.

Since there seemed no immediate danger, he continued his journey, parting company with the tracks and searching for the elusive bit scent. He didn't find any. Disappointed he prowled further away, spotting a bou, but not daring to try and take it down by himself. Better to hunt the rightful prey with his siblings.

Pausing to take a drink from a crack in the ice, he jerked his head up, his ears listening. The faint sound was like nothing he knew. Curious, he followed the elusive noise until he reached a steep cliff. A vast crevasse spread out below him. Jagged boulders protruded from the sides and scraggly white barked trees bent to the will of the slow moving ice.

Dermot considered trying to find a way down and finally decided not to. He'd been away from the pack long enough. Returning the same way he'd come, he chanced upon a bit and gave chase. The small fast moving bit proved to be quicker and disappeared down a hole.

Upset he was returning with no meat, Dermot slowly trudged back. Several body lengths from the den, he spotted tracks. Not the ones the amber had left. These were different. They sank deep in the snow and looked to be long and continuous.

No predator or prey he knew of left such marks!

Barking he raced to warn his pack about this new invader. When he reached the clearing, he found the spot deserted. Other tracks mixed with his siblings and he smelled blood. He leaped over a long log and discovered the body of one of brothers. A large hole leaked red over his brother's muzzle and stained the ivory snow.

A body length away he found the death scent of a creature he didn't know. There was no carcass or bones, so either it had been dragged away by scavengers or else the invaders took their dead with them. Where that thought had come from, he didn't know. His kind always left the bodies of the dead where they had fallen. Others would come and feast leaving no trace.

In honor of his brother, he raised his head and howled. The sound bounced between the peaks and rose as a plea to Wepwawet. His prayer asked the fierce god to take the soul of the one fallen in battle and welcome him as one who had rightfully died protecting the pack.

When his plea had been completed, he tried to discover where the others had gone. He sniffed around the edges of the clearing trying to find their track. Mixed with theirs was a smell he didn't know and soon his nose lost the trail completely.

~ * ~

"And then what happened?" Jyotis asked. She rested across the strange fur, her white black spotted front paws before her, her limber back ones stretched lazily behind her.

Dermot rose and walked to one of the containers set in the floor. He drank and resettled himself on the edge of the fur.

"I...alone..."

~ * ~

Alone and not able to find his pack, Dermot debated on what to do next. Obviously his leaders had taken great care to make certain the invaders could not follow them. Unfortunately, their cunning had also lost him.

He again tried to find them, scouring the edges of the clearing, working slowly several body lengths away, frantically trying to find a scent, any scent that would lead him to his brothers and sisters.

The sun sagged over the mountain peaks and he finally admitted to himself he would not be able to find them. He slept the darkness away in the hollow den intended for the puppies and when the sun rose he left the familiar clearing.

He followed the stream down the mountain until his stomach ached and he knew he had to hunt. A small bit darted from behind a rock and he dined on it. He drank his fill from the cold water and kept going.

Flakes began to fall around him. Instinct instructed he should take shelter. He chose not to and began to run. White obscured his sight and he could no longer see the stream he used as his guide. Still he ran.

And ran. And ran.

He ran until his legs wobbled. His fur, though thick enough to protect him from the bitter cold, now was soaked and he shivered. Looking around for a place to rest and be protected from the storm, the heavy thickness hid any possible refuge.

Slowly he moved to one side, trying to find the stream. He couldn't. The memories of his ancestors surfaced and he acted on the thought. His front paws dug into the deep snow and he buried himself.

He didn't know how long he slept in the snow. When he awoke, he panicked at first, not remembering what he had done. Frantically he freed himself and shook ice crystals from his fur. Now he saw the storm had stopped. The sun reflected brightly, the dazzling light blinding him.

Dermot didn't find anything familiar in the steep valley, not even the stream. He continued on knowing his only chance of survival depended on not stopping, finding water and perhaps a bit.

~ * ~

The two-legged invaders seemed to have left. Rowena and one of her brothers, Naois, trailed the deep tracks for several sunrises. When they returned they told us the metal monster had gone further into the old city. The creatures had intently searched the old twisted skyscrapers, then headed out across the endless white plains.

At least I would not have to come up with a plan to defend my den right away. Relieved, I played wrestling games with my kittens and continued to teach them reading skills as they went on to more difficult books.

Algier taught the Sciences and I found myself tensing when he watched Sasha. My foundling was growing quickly, and I knew soon, she would come into her first heat. I had no doubt he would challenge me for her.

"He's been told she's intended for you," Starlite said. She seemed to sense my anxiety. She jumped off the counter and onto the chair beside me.

I lazily turned my head to look at her. Such a beauty! I still marveled that I had won her.

"He's an unattached male," I responded. "I knew he might challenge."

"Algier has been told not to," she repeated. Affectionately she licked my muzzle.

"Doesn't matter when a female comes into heat." I knew the madness that overcame a male. The driving need to fight and mate.

"I'll run him off myself if he challenges you."

"I need another male to help defend the den."

"You don't need another to challenge your right of dominance."

She was right. Yet so was I. An idea came to me. "Perhaps you should suggest to your brother he go to the male gatherings. Find himself a female and bring her here."

"I have. He wants Sasha."

"She's not his to have." I also remembered I had promised her the right to choose for herself. When she came into heat, would I allow her to?

Starlite bumped me with her head. I touched her nose. She snuggled against me and we shared warmth during our nap. She left when she awoke to take her kittens hunting. They were going outside for lessons on stalking rabbit.

I jumped down and stretched my large body. Rowena rose and barked hopefully, her tail wagging. Leisurely I strolled across the tattered rug and down the dusty hallway. The wolf's nails clicked behind me.

At the entrance I breathed in the cold air. A storm had passed over us leaving an unmarred sloped hill. To one side I saw the tracks of Starlite and her kittens. They had gone around the building towards the rabbit-hunting field.

"Hi, Daddy!" Nan hopped like a rabbit past me and over to the edge. "Come on, Jojo!"

The younger wolf leaped out pulling a piece of rug. He placed in on the ground and Nan climbed on. With a push of his nose he sent my kitten down the slope. The rag stopped at the bottom. Nan jumped off. "Again!"

"They found a book talking about the human children doing something called sledding." Lara stood beside me. Her three kittens ran out and joined in the fun. Jojo pulled the rag back up and Hardy took a turn, then Stirling and Trotsky.

"It's good for them to find a way to play," Lara mused. She sat down, her thick black tail resting across her white paws.

"Rowena and I are going to hunt."

"It would be nice to have a flapper. Goose," she corrected herself as her copper eyes met mine. "But a rabbit will do."

"I'll see what I can find." I headed out the other direction, across the small plain and past the other buildings I was certain had once also been part of the school. Odd metal shapes greeted me as I crossed the area. I think it was once the playground.

My journey took me under the broken wooden fence and back into the houses that humans had once inhabited. I had explored some of them in the past. Useful strips of wool and other warm fabrics I had brought back. Sometimes, I even found books. Often though, my searches yielded nothing.

Dodging under a fallen tree, something dashed out of a small outside house and charged me. Rowena leaped over me and confronted the attacker. I retreated back under the tree and watched the battle.

The attacker was a very large sniffer or dog as I had learned. The two circled, growling. The dog lunged for the neck and Rowena dodged. She darted back and grabbed his neck. I heard a loud snap and the dog's body went limp. The wolf shook it a couple of times and dumped the limp body on the ground.

Concern for Starlite and her kittens overwhelmed me. They were hunting in the field and open to attack. Where one dog was, there were always more. I ran back to the school, Rowena easily loping beside me.

"Lara!" I called. "Dogs! Get the kittens back inside and tell the others!"

I saw the Maine Coon dash out and end the sledding fun. Continuing on I hoped I was not too late. I prayed to The Provider to protect my mate and our kittens.

I dashed through the pines and past the crumbling houses. I strained my ears. Faintly I heard the barks of dogs and made myself run faster. Rowena and I finally broke through the last of the old neighborhood and I frantically searched the broad plain for Starlite.

Many body lengths away I could see her. She'd backed her kittens against a stump and stood protectively in front of them, her fur fluffed high, one of her paws striking out at the dog gang that circled around. All I thought about was getting to her and protecting my family.

I yowled my rage, ready to fight to the death. Rowena gently pushed me to one side and I hissed at her. She yipped strongly, again nudging me aside.

I saw the movement over the snow. White and splotched shadows creeping slowly around the dog gang. Black and brown streaked over the stump and confronted the dog leader. Snarls filled the air.

My heart beat very fast. What about Starlite and my kittens? It was my job to protect them. There had to be a way!

The large wolf pushed the canine leader back. I recognized a second shape creeping around the stump. Lavena! The dominant female stood over my mate and our kittens protectively.

The black and brown wolf had to be the dominant male. The rest of the pack had now cut off any possible retreat for the gang. The two leaders lunged at each other and a fierce fight ensued. I saw nothing but blurs of fur and splattering red blood!

Chapter 11

Anumati lifted her head and regarded the howler. He'd fallen silent and not continued his story. She still didn't know how he'd come to speak her tongue.

"So what happened then?" Valmiki sat close to her haunches. He scratched his ear with his oversized paw and swatted at Kerani's tail. She hissed in retaliation.

The howler, Dermot, she reminded herself, gazed longingly at the pair. His blue eyes blinked and his tail wagged briefly.

"Long…journey…"

～ * ～

His stomach seemed to have attached itself to his ribs. No bits had crossed his trail for several sunrises and his only water had been mouths full of snow. Dermot raised his head and sniffed, a lonely howl escaping his muzzle.

The sound traveled with the wind down the long valley and out into the sky. Perhaps Wepwawet would be merciful and take him in death. That fate would be much better than being separated from the pack surrounded by silence and not his siblings.

No, not total silence. The sound reaching him reminded him of a branch breaking. Under his paws the ground shook and he looked up. Above his head the snow once covering the steep slopes tumbled downward.

Pure fear filled him and he ran.

～ * ～

I don't know how long the fight took. When all the dogs were dead, the wolves barked rejoicing, their victory turning to howls of mournful loss. The dominant male had died in battle. His mate lay beside him and the rest of the pack surrounded them. I crept in gathering up Starlite, Neutron and Sapphire and we returned to my den.

Rowena didn't return for several sunrises. She crept in as the sun blazed in red and pink glory behind the mountains. She and Jojo woofed far into the dark, Nan and Mitzy sitting with them.

Mitzy found me as the sun rose. "The wolves have chosen a new dominant male."

The warm sun felt good on my body. I'd chosen to stretch out on the windowsill. "Does this affect our relationship with the pack?"

"Yes and no." My Calico mate joined me licking one her paws. "As I understand it, the second male becoming their new pack leader wasn't a surprise. Rowena and Jojo, or Kayne as the pack calls him, can continue to stay here. What has changed," she laid down with her front paws tucked under her torso, "is that the wolves are going to move into one of the buildings near the school. They want the pups educated. Besides," her tail twitched, "after the incident with the dogs and the strange metal monster, Herne thinks we should all be closer together so we can help protect each other."

I knew Starlite and our kittens would not still be alive if the wolves hadn't come. In fact, I would probably have died as well leaving my family unprotected and open for domination by a new male, which undoubtedly, would have been Midnight. He still left urine marks for me to find.

"How soon and which building?" I wanted to know. There were three to choose from.

"Within a few sunrises," Mitzy replied. "They'll take the most intact one, which they've already explored. The other two have missing walls and roofs."

That meant the one closest. There seemed to be some sort of ramp leading to the door. I hadn't been inside any of them, but the windows were still intact and thick fabric hung over them.

"They'll be welcome here. I didn't get a chance to tell the pack thank you."

"Nan and I will need to help you teach the pups."

"I think the two of you can teach them. Nan is doing just fine with Jojo."

"Word Warrior, you too need to learn the wolf tongue."

Mitzy was right. If the pack leader, Herne she'd called him, thought it necessary for us to live closer together to survive, then the least I could do was speak to him in his own tongue.

"Will you teach me?" I blinked my turquoise eyes.

She contemplated before she answered. "Of course."

~ * ~

When next he opened his eyes, Dermot found himself in a cave. Slowly he staggered up, wincing at his sore paws. Dampness mixed with mold tickled his nose and he sneezed. He trotted to the entrance wanting to discover where he was, since he had no memory of how he got there.

From the entrance he could see the long valley below. Sun glistened off white. Busted green pines lay like bones everywhere. Huge boulders had broken through the ice and water gurgled around them.

"It is good you found this refuge."

He whirled around, his teeth bared and a deep growl in his throat.

The Spotted Ghost stared at him steadily, its tail slowly swinging. "No doubt you wonder how I speak your tongue."

He had wondered actually, uncertain if the Ghost was a threat or not. The packs generally kept to themselves. None of the tales he'd heard had said anything about the Ghosts being intelligent. Or even that they could speak to the wolves.

"I am called Indrani. My mother named me so. I am the Wise One, Keeper of the Knowledge."

"What knowledge?" Since she hadn't jumped him, he knew she was female from the tits he finally saw, he relaxed slightly, but not entirely. The Ghost might still attack him.

"How we came to be in this land so far from the high peaks where our ancestors roamed and hunted."

He was beginning to lose interest. How they came to be here was of no consequence to him. "How do you speak my tongue?"

"In this valley, I am known as a healer. Even the packs come. I had to learn to speak with them."

Even the packs came? Why hadn't his pack known? Many times they'd wished to help an injured member, only to watch them die in pain. If they'd known about Indrani, maybe…he pushed the memory aside. He didn't want to remember how his sister died.

"I killed a horned one, a bou you call them. You can share my meat."

His attention focused back on her. She'd offered to share her meat? His stomach rumbled and his hunger surfaced full force. Following her deep into the cave she showed him her kill and she jumped up to pine boughs sitting on a high ledge.

He hesitated briefly and began to gobble down bites, even as he warily kept watch on her. She ignored him, bathing her paws and grooming her face. When he finally ate his fill, he drank from the small clear pool against a long column.

"You are welcome to stay." She blinked at him.

After his nap he was restless to continue, yet the soreness of his paws prevented him from running away from this strange Ghost. He laid down on the cold ground, resting his head between his front legs.

Indrani jumped down and sniffed his paws. "You're hurt." She padded away returning soon. She licked at something she'd brought back and her tongue rasped over his paws. The tingling pain eased. "Rest," she gently ordered.

~ * ~

I watched from the entrance as the wolves moved into the small tan building. Lara stood beside me. They'd come just as the moon rose into the black sky. Nan bounded across the snow, Jojo beside her.

"They say the building is cozy and they're gonna be very happy living there," she informed me.

Jojo sat, his long tongue hanging out of his mouth. Nan hopped around him. He lifted a paw and stopped her, pushing her to the ground. She wiggled free and the two rushed past us in a game of chase.

"It's good they're friends," Lara observed. She licked a paw and washed her black face.

"Yes," I agreed. Wind tumbled around us scooping up the new powder and blowing it in our faces. I retreated back inside. Lara followed.

"Starlite told me Algier attended the last male gathering."

I knew already. She'd told me when her brother left, and when he'd returned. We entered the library. Many of my kittens were sprawled around the room, some reading, some playing, others lounging on the windowsills.

"He says there are stories coming down the mountain about a Spotted Ghost with cubs."

Jumping up on the chair I circled and settled my muscled body on the cushion. Lara joined me, bathing my head. I enjoyed her attention and affectionately rubbed along the side of her face.

"Word Warrior," she pulled away, "none of the Spotted Ghosts have come down so far. The males are worried."

"Probably just hunting for her young. I don't think we need worry about them."

"What if you're wrong? What, if food is scarce and she's coming to the valley to hunt? We're the right size to be her prey."

"Lara," I touched her nose with mine. "Please, don't worry. I'm sure the wolves will help defend us if it looks like the Spotted Ghost is a danger."

"You hope," she muttered, curling so her back was to me.

~ * ~

He woke in the morning feeling rested. He again ate some of the bou and drank from the pool. Dermot did notice his feet didn't hurt anymore.

"You're feeling better?" Indrani joined him.

"Yes. Thank you."

"Many of us who walk on four paws are rising to intelligence," she commented, leaping up to her bed of boughs.

Somehow, a part of him knew what she was saying was important. He gingerly climbed the tiered rock until he stood so he could see her clearly.

"I think," her tail flicked, "it is important we can communicate. I speak your tongue, but you do not speak mine. You should learn." Her yellow eyes met his blue ones. "If you wish, I can teach you."

Did he want to learn? He considered her words. If he ever found his pack again, knowing she could help them meant better survival. Convincing the dominants might be a problem, but once they understood knowing Indrani would be an advantage to the pack, well, maybe it would advance him.

She snorted. "Many such as yourself separate from the pack. They wander on and begin new packs. Perhaps you should think about that."

His own pack? Dermot hadn't considered the possibility. Maybe he could convince a female to mate with him and then *he* could be the dominant male. His tail wagged in excitement.

"Now," Indrani rose and stretched her long body. "Let us begin your lessons."

~ * ~

So another of Anumati's kind, a Wise One at that, had taught Dermot their language. And convinced him to think about starting his own pack?

"Mama, I'm hungry," Kerani complained.

Valmiki retorted, "It's still snowing. You wouldn't find anything to hunt out there. Our prey is at least smart enough to hide someplace warm."

Kerani glared at her brother and looked out the door. Huge flakes fell thickly. "Doesn't mean I'm not hungry."

"There will be many times in your life you will be hungry," Anumati sadly told her daughter. "Sometimes prey are difficult to find, and you could go many sunrises without a full belly."

Kerani lay down next to her sister who had finally fallen asleep. She put her head down and closed her eyes. Valmiki joined them.

"Life...lesson....hard...teach...cubs..."

"But they'll learn or die."

"True."

"Dermot, we're going into the valley to take Snow Fur," she gazed at the small white lump cuddled next to her, "to the feline who reads."

"I...go...with...you."

She hadn't thought about that. She'd assumed he'd leave when the storm stopped.

"Packs...valley...I ...help...you."

Anumati didn't know there were howlers in the valley. She'd assumed they were all in the mountains. Maybe having him along would insure their survival. He could ask the packs in the valley about the feline and help get them there safely.

"You can come with us."

"Good." He laid down his head.

She also closed her eyes but didn't sleep. The wind shook the roof and cold air seeped into their shelter. Her cubs, one by one, rearranged themselves around her, sharing her warmth. Finally, she slept.

~ * ~

Dermot's low growl reached her ears forcing her to wake. She half opened her eyes to see what potential threat he warned about.

Long claws reached around the edge, followed by the short nose of a swiper!

Anumati slowly got to her feet and crept close to Dermot. She put her muzzle against his long ear. "I will distract the swiper and led it away. After I leave, take my cubs and Snow Fur to the valley and the feline who reads."

A huffing sound echoed in their small shelter. She continued. "Don't wait for me to come back. If I lose, the swiper will return. I don't want my cubs killed."

"Understand." Dermot backed against the wall, giving her more room.

"Mama," Kerani protested.

"Remember my example. You may have to do the same for your cubs. Obey Dermot."

With that final order she yowled a loud challenge and scratched the swiper's nose. Sharp talons swung at her and she retreated out of the predator's reach. Judging the distance carefully, she leaped past the huge creature. Black eyes of the very large swiper followed her movements. Blood dripped down its short nose onto its white fur.

Snow blew fiercely obscuring the structure where they'd sheltered. Anumati sent a prayer to Sekhmet asking for strength and wisdom to defeat the potential threat, and to urge the swiper to go after her, and not her cubs.

The swiper sent one final glance backward and lumbered swiftly after her. She headed back up the valley, pausing to make certain the predator had not returned below.

She hissed and kept going until she reached a spot where she felt she had the best advantage. The sheer rock of the mountain guarded her back. She whirled and met the swiper who stood on its hind legs and advanced on her.

Snarling she enticed it forward. The battle they fought was short and fierce. At the end, the swiper hooked into her back and broke her spine. Her last prayer to Sekhmet was of thanks for sparing Anumati's cubs, and Snow Fur.

~ * ~

Dermot didn't wait long before forcing the cubs out into the storm. He wondered how to transport the small feline, but Valmiki solved the problem by coaching Snow Fur onto the cub's strong back. To his eyes, the sight of the solid white on black spotted fur was strange. Valmiki looked like he had a sick growth.

Pushing such unpleasant thoughts away, he led the way down to the lake's edge. Hesitantly he put his paws on the frozen surface. It wasn't that he hadn't crossed such before, he just hoped no sudden holes appeared and swallowed up him, or his new charges.

When the snow fell so thick he could no longer see, he chose a direction, hoping his god proved kind. He needed to find shelter to wait it out. Wepwawet must have taken pity on him for suddenly before them was a wooden shelter. He waited at the entrance as the cubs went in first. He entered himself after making sure they all were there.

Some of the logs had fallen yet the small place seemed mostly intact. An old stone structure stood in the middle of the room and reached to the top. Soft places to bed down were set all around. The females chose their spots curling up together on the largest piece and drying each other with their tongues.

Snow Fur jumped off Valmiki's back and quickly dried himself. When he finished the small cub began to explore the place.

"Don't…go…far…" Dermot instructed.

"He can't hear you," Valmiki reminded him between licks.

Of course. The Ghost female had told him. Still it was odd. In the pack, a defective cub would have been left to die.

"I doubt he'll go far." The young male plopped down on the dirty floor.

Dermot walked a few body lengths away and shook vigorously. Once dry he noticed a way up to the higher level. His nails clicked on his chosen path and once above he found a number of rooms.

"What's up here?" Valmiki poked his head into one of the rooms.

The wolf explored the second room. Soft, warm places to sleep lured him and he claimed one for himself. Not long afterward something bounced up next to him. He opened one tired eye as Snow Fur curled up by his side. A heavier weight joined him as well.

"My sisters are asleep," Valmiki told him, "and I didn't want to wake them."

With the combined warmth of the two felines reminding him of happier days with the pack, Dermot allowed himself to drift to sleep.

Chapter 12

I lazed on the windowsill wishing the sun burned bright to warm my body and marveling at the changes over the past three full moons. Lavena's two daughters had also decided they wanted their cubs educated and had, like their mother, chosen closer dens.

Yseult and her mate Sloan, had chosen one of the farthest classrooms for their pack and their two young pups. Cara and Phelan had wanted the gym, but Algier had chased them out. The pair finally chose the classroom facing the coldest winds. They had three young.

Stretching one leg, I glanced down at the lessons in progress. Mitzy and Nan, with the help of Jojo and Rowena, taught the seven wolf cubs. Lara had her small group of kittens discovering more secrets of numbers and Algier's few huddled around one of the large books I'd brought back from the library. The rest of my kittens were either reading or else chasing each other around metal chair legs and over the dusty counters.

Outside the snow fell thickly. I'd heard, now that Algier went to the male meetings, that the strange metal monster had not returned. Yet, there were more stories of another rattling creature up in the mountains. Had I been foolish to think there had been only one? What if the other came back here? I still hadn't come up with a plan to protect my females and kittens.

"And what are you so seriously thinking about?" Tomura gracefully arched up and settled beside me, gazing through the ice filmed window.

"Wondering what to do if the metal monster returns."

"Hiding seemed to work." Her thin tail beat slightly against the sill.

"They weren't really looking for us." I sat up.

"Yes. I do wonder what they wanted with that…thing."

I didn't know. Vividly I remembered when it had howled and hurt our ears. It had been silent since then. Still, I didn't know what it was and nothing in the books I'd found had told me.

"How's Callie?"

Our Elder hadn't left her room since all the wolves had moved in. After the sun set, my kittens joined her for stories. Even Mitzy's were in attendance despite the fact Callie had sworn not to include them.

Tomura cleaned a spot on her shoulder. "We hunt for her food and leave choice bits. Starlite is with her now." My mate rubbed against my muzzle. "Come hunt with me."

Together we leaped down and headed through the dark cold hallway. Squeaks reached my ears and I paused, trying to locate the direction of the sound. We chased several of the rodents before each catching one. We returned to Tomura's room and ate our meal, leaving some for her kittens.

"When the storm stops I'll go hunt for rabbit." I licked dried brakish blood off my paw.

"I will need to take my kittens to the field and instruct them." Tomura finished cleaning her face.

"Have you spoken with Sasha about her first heat?"

"I have. She understands males will come to fight for her. My daughter does not want to leave." She blinked her slanted chocolate eyes. "Sasha does not like Algier."

Algier's interest had become more blatant. Sasha hissed and ran away from him constantly.

"Starlite has spoken to her brother. He doesn't want to listen." I sensed a challenge might be coming between the two of us.

"He may need to be run off." She stretched her long sleek back. "I will not tolerate another male challenging you for her."

"Yet I may have to fight many other males for her."

"You are an excellent fighter."

"True. But I haven't fought any challenges lately." I had as many females as I wanted and no desire to add any more. Besides, the other males resented me and I no longer was welcome at their meetings nor did I hear about desirable females coming into their seasons. Even Algier didn't tell me.

"It will be well, Word Warrior." My mate's warm rumble soothed me. "Come. Rest with me."

I curled next to her in her warm nest and she cleaned around my ears. She continued to purr as I fell into a restless sleep.

~ * ~

When Dermot woke he discovered the two female cubs had joined them. They must have either gotten lonely or cold. He didn't know which. Snow Fur lifted his head and blinked blue eyes at the wolf.

"Wonder why you're so important she'd protect you," Dermot mused.

If he hadn't been asked to protect her cubs and Snow Fur, he would have chosen to abandon the small feline. He wondered if it might not be best for them all if he did.

After all, their survival might depend on not having to carry or hunt for the helpless cat. If another ambler appeared, they might all have to run. He doubted Snow Fur would be able to stay on Valmiki's back. Maybe he should just take the feline outside and break its neck.

Snow Fur stretched and put his paw on Dermot's side. The wolf gazed down still debating on what to do.

"Mama wanted us to go to the feline who reads," Jyotis said, her head resting on the wolf's back. "Are you going to take us there now?"

"Since she asked me to, yes."

"Snow Fur came from another valley. Howlers brought him to us to raise."

That surprised him. Those like him, since he understood the Ghosts called them Howlers, had brought the feline to the Spotted Ghost female? All thoughts about killing Snow Fur left. If others of his kind had thought the small cat important enough to bring to another larger one to raise, then he must abide by their decision.

"I'm hungry," Kerani complained.

"You're always hungry." Valmiki's heavy paws hit the surface with a thud.

Dermot glanced through the strangely protected windows. Snow still heavily fell. There would be no hunting for bit or bou.

"Let's explore!" Jyotis joined her brother and the two ran out of the room.

Kerani rolled into a tight ball and didn't move. The wolf left her there and went briefly outside to relieve himself. When he came back in he found the two cubs eating small rodents.

"There's many of them in there." Valmiki padded to a dark ragged hole.

Not knowing exactly what they were, he almost hesitated. Hunger won out and he caught two of them and had a fine meal.

He did notice Snow Fur had joined the two cubs. Jyotis tore off small chunks of meat for him. The cat ate and when he finished he went to the stone thing to play.

"I'll go tell Kerani about these!" Valmiki raced up to where his sister still slept.

Dermot lay on the floor while Jyotis sprawled on one of the soft things. Snow Fur tired of playing and joined the cub. She washed him and after, the two fell asleep, the smaller feline tucked between Jyotis' paws, as he'd seen their mother do.

Kerani finally came down. Her brother showed her where the rodents were. She caught one and ate it. "Not as good as a large foot."

"At least we can eat while we're here." Valmiki claimed a soft place. "We're not leaving until the storm stops. Are we?"

"No." Dermot put his head on his paws. He missed his pack and he wondered if he'd ever see them again. Being with the ghost cubs was not the same as his brothers and sisters.

"Do you think mama will find us?" Kerani stood before him, her long tail swaying brushing against the wood floor and causing dust to swirl around her feet.

"If can." He was pretty certain if she hadn't found them already, she wouldn't find them at all. A part of him sensed she was probably dead. Few survived a battle with an ambler.

"I wanted to stay in our den."

"We're too young to be on our own. Mama told us," Valmiki reminded his sister.

Her head popped up proudly. "I can hunt."

"We all can." Valmiki yawned. "But there are other things we need to learn. Like about matings."

"Like I care about that." She went back up to where they'd slept during the dark.

"You will!" her brother called after her.

"What do, if no return?" Dermot couldn't stop the question.

"We won't survive," Valmiki truthfully replied.

The simple truth cut like sharp teeth. Anumati had charged him with getting Snow Fur to the valley and taking care of her cubs. Yet he didn't know anything about raising young Spotted Ghosts. In the pack, everyone raised the puppies. How was he supposed to manage alone?

~ * ~

Midnight had been here again. I found his marking on the side of the school when I'd gone out to relieve myself at sunrise. No doubt he knew a female was soon coming into heat and wanted his intentions known. Not that I would allow *him* to win Sasha.

The storm dropped heavy wet flakes. Venturing out would probably be a mistake, yet I had tired of being inside. Besides, Tomura complained she didn't want rat anymore and couldn't I go find her a tasty rabbit?

Pushing against the wind with the cold starting to claw through my thick fur, I went down the hill and through the pines. Broken fences crossed my path and I easily slipped though the gaps. After the second hill, the rabbit hunting place finally appeared.

I stopped to rest and watch for them. None were out. No doubt they were secure and warm in their deep holes. I knew they would not be out again until the storm passed.

Returning the same way, I went back to the school and her room. Tomura looked expectantly at me from her perch on the windowsill. "No rabbits?" Her disappointed eyes bore into me. She turned away and stared outside.

I continued down the hall to the library. The wolf cubs weren't here. Jojo and Nan studied a book and Rowena lifted her head when I entered.

"No rabbits, huh, Daddy?" Nan sounded unhappy.

"They're hiding. They won't come out until after the snow stops."

"Mama told me you had goose once. Do you think you'll ever find another one?"

"I don't know."

"Daddy? How'd this awful long winter get started?"

"We don't know. Even my Elders never told us stories about why it happened."

"Guess Callie wouldn't know then." Nan nestled against Jojo. He made a noise I'd not heard before and wagged his tail.

"Where are the other kittens?" Normally they were all over the library.

"Mostly with their mothers. Sasha is reading one of the books you brought back. I think she's on a shelf."

Well, I could understand my kittens cuddling with their mothers. The bitter cold seemed to be seeping into the building. Which reminded me, I sat down and quickly dried myself.

Starlite raced in. "Word Warrior! Come quickly!"

I followed my silver colored mate down the hall and into the small room Callie occupied. Our Elder lay tightly curled in her warm wool nest.

"Callie!" Starlite nudged the one who'd raised her. Her worried blue eyes met mine. "I can't get her to wake up!"

I heard rapidly clicking nails and caught the tip of Rowena's white tail as the wolf ran from the room. Vaguely I'd been aware of her following us from the library. Starlite licked Callie's nose.

"Her nose is hot!"

With a sinking dread I contemplated my next words. When healthy our noses are cold and wet usually, though not always. When we're sick, they can become hot and dry. I had no idea what was wrong with Callie, but I feared we might lose our Elder.

Lavena pushed her way into the room. Her two daughters stood in the narrow door. The female sniffed Callie and barked some instructions. Yseult whirled around and left while Cara curled her canine body around our ill Elder.

I had no idea what was going on. Neither Mitzy nor Nan were here to translate and I still hadn't yet mastered the basics of the wolf tongue.

Starlite came to stand beside me. "What are they doing?"

"Trying to help." Or at least, I hoped they were.

Yseult returned shortly with some bark in her mouth. Lavena took it, chewed and put the mixture around Callie's mouth. Our Elder's tongue slowly cleaned the stuff away, although she never opened her eyes.

Lavena again barked and Yseult left. The dominant female also curled around Callie.

"There isn't much we can do," I told Starlite.

"I know." Her troubled eyes met mine and looked away.

"You stay." I knew my mate would anyway. Callie, even though our Elder hadn't birthed Starlite, was the only mother she'd known.

Starlite hesitantly approached the two wolves. Lavena made room for her and my mate joined them.

Leaving the room, I felt helpless. I hadn't found any information in the human books about illness. I didn't know what to do.

Chapter 13

Dermot woke from his nap, listening to the thumping sound of Valmiki's paws on the wooden upward path. His blue eyes watched the young cub drop a brown object onto the floor, which Snow Fur immediately took.

"What that?" He raised his white head.

"Snow Fur found it between the logs. He wouldn't leave until I pulled it out and brought it here."

The small cub pushed it open with his nose. Pale crinkled things reminding Dermot of dead pine needles but less pleasant smelling, lay before Snow Fur. He examined the object with complete attention, his tail tip slowly flipping.

"He won't do anything else except look at it," Valmiki told Dermot. "Snow Fur had lots of those back in our den. Mama always knew what he found was important, even if she never understood why."

An idea sprang into the wolf's mind. Anumati was sending the tiny cub into the valley to be with the feline who could read. Maybe, just maybe, Snow Fur already knew how!

Dermot didn't know how many sunrises passed before the thick snow stopped. He stood at the entrance of their shelter sniffing the cold wind. The scent told him they had many sunsets before another storm came. It was time to move on.

He went back inside. "Time go."

Jyotis and Valmiki immediately sprang up, with Snow Fur taking his perch on the young male's back. The male cub also took the brown object into his mouth.

"Snow Fur won't leave unless we take it with us," Jyotis explained.

The wolf didn't know if taking the object was wise. It might slow them down.

"I don't want to leave," Kerani objected. She still sat on one of the soft places.

"You not ready…be on own."

"I have everything I need. A place to den and good meat."

"But you'd be all alone," Jyotis replied sadly.

"Mama always told us as we spend most of our lives alone."

"Kerani...come."

"No."

Valmiki put the object on the floor. "Kerani, stop being foolish. Come with us to the valley."

"You go to the valley." She jumped down and turned away.

Dermot didn't know what to do. Anumati had wanted him to look after her cubs. Their mother had known they weren't old enough to be on their own. He went after her.

She spun around snarling and raised her sharp claws in warning. "I never wanted to leave our den. I don't want to leave the mountains. Just take my brother and sister and leave me here."

"You want...die...like your mother."

"Better to die then to go with a howler!"

He snapped at her, nipping her other front paw. She leaped at him. He prepared for her heavy weight to hit, and when it did, the two rolled across the gritty floor.

"Stop it, Kerani!" Valmiki hissed. "Mama told us to go with Dermot! She told us to obey him!"

The young female pulled away. The wolf backed up, wary and breathing hard. He could feel long scratches along his side, but they were shallow and would heal quickly.

"I don't care! I'm not leaving!" She sprang out another entrance and disappeared into thick pines.

Dermot considered going after her. He took one step forward and changed his mind. He still had two of the cubs and Snow Fur. And he had been charged with keeping them safe.

"Are you going to go after my sister?" Jyotis asked, her voice scared.

"No. Some wolves leave pack. Never return. Kerani wanted to go. I let her."

"She won't survive," Valmiki informed him.

"Maybe. We go to valley."

~ * ~

Many sunrises later they reached the place with stinky water. The stench reminded Dermot of the bad eggs he'd found once. He'd thought to have a rare treat for a meal and instead, when he'd stepped on one, he'd spent many sunrises trying to get the stench out of his nose.

"Yuck!" Jyotis wrinkled her muzzle.

"Warm though." Dermot lead the way into the wooden shelter.

Steam and smell laced the dark wood walls. Many small pools surrounded by smooth rocks sat in the hard floor. One side had a clear wall giving a good view of the small mountain valley. Pines still heavy from the storm sagged under the weight.

Snow Fur jumped off Valmiki's back. He sniffed, sneezed, and jumped up onto one of the many odd structures in the room. The little male curled his white tail around his paws and blinked blue eyes.

Valmiki put the brown object beside Snow Fur and padded around. Jyotis joined him. The two cubs explored the many pools, extending their paws into the water and rapidly pulling them out.

Dermot watched them for awhile and went further into the shelter. They would need something soft to sleep on. Sharp noises reminding him of when the pack spoke together reached his long ears.

Carefully he stalked the source, taking pride in his ability to hide well and not be seen. After trotting down a long dark tunnel, he peered around the edge.

In another room, long rock reaching to the top, a fire blazed. Several bright creatures huddled around it, reaching pale paws toward the warmth. A big one joined them, walking on two legs, putting a long thing reminding him of a tree trunk, down.

Some deep warning sense burned inside him and Dermot silently backed away. He retreated back down the dark tunnel to the place of stinky water.

"No stay. Danger."

"What kind of danger?" Valmiki asked.

"Not know. We leave."

Quickly they left the place and returned to the growing dark. The sun sank rapidly behind the gathering clouds. The scent told Dermot another storm was coming.

"Where are we going?" Jyotis walked beside him.

Odd colorful wooden shelters met his eyes. He waited until the end of them and chose a long narrow one. It had many clear walls revealing the steep mountain cliffs behind as well as a clear view in every direction. That would give him the added security of being able to see any two legged invaders if they by chance, came this way.

He entered the shelter. Many smaller clear walls were inside. Over to one side, a room with a wall down the middle gave them a place to hide. To Dermot's surprise, there were soft places for them to sleep, even if they were chilly.

The cubs managed to curl up together and Snow Fur joined them. Dermot napped, keeping his ears sharply alert to any sound of danger.

When the sun rose next, pitched squeaks that hurt his ears woke him. The wolf skulked across the cold torn up floor and carefully checked outside. Several two-legged creatures and some sort of yellow monster were outside.

He noticed the tracks and his heart beat fast. They were the same he'd seen when he'd tried to return to his pack!

"What are those?" Valmiki stared curiously through the clear wall.

"Danger. We leave. Now."

"But what are they?"

"Come." He nipped the cub's foot in warning to force obedience.

The young male snarled in response but obeyed. They rejoined Jyotis and Snow Fur. Dermot heard crunching noises and feared the creatures might be coming inside.

"Danger. We go."

He led the way out a swinging entrance and through a place with long gray ledges piled with hollow rocks and green springy fungus. Another entrance with a broken hanging cover presented itself. He dashed outside, scrambling up a steep high bank and down into a small valley.

Once again he found himself on frozen water. He made sure the cubs followed before using it like a well marked trail. They passed many scattered wooden shelters. Snow began to fall and he hoped it would cover their tracks.

"Are we going to find a cave or something?" Jyotis shivered.

"Soon."

The frozen water passed through a cave. They had temporary respite from the blowing wind and wet flakes. When they emerged he kept going, the pressing need to put as much distance between them and the two-legs as possible. He kept moving despite his instincts insisting they needed to find shelter and wait out the storm.

He left the water path and began to climb. Pines would shelter them from sight. He finally stopped under a thick branch, which offered some protection from the blowing cold and snow. The cubs crawled in next to him. They all curled up together to keep warm and to wait out the storm.

~ * ~

Several sunrises later I stopped my reading when I heard Callie's yowl and several startled yelps. Running down the hall I encountered Yseult and Cara cowering just outside our Elder's door. Entering the room I discovered Callie hissing, her back arched, and Lavena standing not far away and refusing to run.

"Callie," I said quietly, "you shouldn't hurt Lavena or her daughters. They saved your life."

"It's true, Callie," Starlite confirmed as she joined me. "Your nose was hot and dry. If it hadn't been for the wolves you'd be greeting Bast."

"Better to greet the goddess then to wake up surrounded by hunters!"

"They're our friends and allies!" I spat back. "It's time you got over your needless fear!"

"You've never had to live in their territory! Or listen to their morning howling!"

"But the wolves never hunted us," Starlite reminded her. "The dogs did."

"A hunter is a hunter. Sniffers are sniffers."

Nan scampered in. "Oh, stop it! Lavena is our friend! Just like Jojo!"

Sun yellow eyes blazed at the kitten, and slowly lifted to me. "You should never have allowed the hunters to come here!"

"In case you've forgotten," Starlite reminded her, "Lavena and her pack saved, not just my life, but also my kittens." She went to Callie. "I'd be dead now if they hadn't chosen to help us. They killed a dog gang."

Callie's orange striped tail whipped back and forth. "I will never trust the hunters."

"Fine," I agreed. "Just don't attack them. We need their help to protect our den."

"We can protect it ourselves," she snapped back.

I knew we couldn't. If the two-legged invaders returned, we'd need the wolve's cunning and fighting skills to defeat the potentially deadly enemy. Since I'd seen them last, I'd learned a lot about some of their suspected past. They'd fought wars for land and other things I didn't quite understand.

"Callie," Starlite warned, "you need to rest. I'll bring you some rat to eat."

"Get these hunters out of here!" our Elder growled.

Nan hacked a phrase and Lavena left, taking her daughters with her.

"You really should be nice to them. They helped you." Nan sat by the door.

Callie ignored her and resettled in her warm bed.

I walked with my daughter back to the library.

She asked me. "Why does Callie hate the wolves so much? They're our friends."

"She lived where the wolves ran. She's afraid of them. I'm not sure why." Jojo ran to meet her and the two took off in a game of chase. I stood in the middle of the large room enjoying the rare quiet. The storm had finally broken and Tomura, Lara and Mitzy had taken most of the kittens outside to hunt. Nan had stayed, as had Sasha. Algier had gone to a male gathering.

I leaped up to the shiny glass object on the counter. Another cat stared back at me. I put my paw against it and felt only hard cold. I cocked my head and wondered. I'd seen mirrors and wondered if this was another, only different.

Jumping down, I went back to the book I'd been reading. It was very thick with words like 'thee' and 'thou'. The words it spoke were oddly comforting, even if I didn't understand most of what it said. Reminded me of when The Provider spoke.

Musing on the concept that maybe the humans had believed something similar, I continued to read.

Light in the room began to dim. I glanced up from reading. My females and kittens would be returning soon. Happiness filled me. I had a very good life. With the wolves joining us we had the beginning of, what did the humans call it, oh, yes, a community.

"Hi, Daddy," Nan bounced into the room. Jojo plodded behind her.

"Been playing?"

"Yes," she sat next to me. "What are you reading?"

"I'm not sure. Some type of human book about maybe, The Provider, who I now believe in."

"Really?" Her yellow eyes examined the page. Jojo poked his nose in it as well.

I left her to read and went to the building entrance. My females and kittens climbed the hill. My nose detected the odor of another storm. A strong part of me was very tired of the endless winter. Many books extolled the wonders of seasons - fall, spring, summer, with leaves on trees and green growing things. How had our world become so cold?

~ * ~

"What do you think, Jojo?" Nan raised her head from the page they'd been reading to look at her littermate. Light was just beginning to filter into the library.

"Not understand much of it."

"Me either. But it seems The Provider loved the humans."

"Time to hunt." Jojo got up and plodded to the door. He paused, waiting for Nan to join him.

Reluctantly she closed the book and looked for a place they could put it so she could read more later. Her Daddy's admission he believed in The Provider surprised her. Her mother preferred Bast.

"Here." Jojo returned and took the book in his mouth. He put it on the shelf.

"Thank you." She batted playfully at him and he chased her out the door and down the hallway.

As they hunted together the words and stories they'd read stayed in her mind. Who was this mysterious god the humans had written of, and why did the words touch her in a way she didn't understand?

~ * ~

My tail flicked as I lazed in the sun on cool concrete and enjoyed the rare somewhat warmer weather. Water dripped from the roof making small pools at irregular points. My females, wives I corrected myself, lay around me, relaxing and yet watchful as our kittens played.

They were taking turns sledding on fabric scrapes. The wolf pups joined in, dragging the worn pieces back up the hill, barking excitedly as my kittens rode down again and again yowling their glee.

From her place beside Tomura, Sasha groomed her gray fur. My daughter hadn't gone into heat when expected and Algier had finally given up waiting. He'd heard in the last male gathering about a promising female several sunrises away. She lived in one of the old stores in a place overlooked by a large rock. Many of the writings mused over the sheer plateau comparing it to a castle. Whatever a castle was.

Midnight had not left any new urine sprays. I suspected the presence of the three wolf packs kept him away. They were presently away hunting deer. Rowena had had been left behind to care for the pups.

Tomura rose and greeted Cleopatra. The two females touched noses as Cleo's kittens raced to join the fun. She'd been the first outside feline to bring her young to me to instruct. At first, my wives had been hostile, but when she made it clear she only wanted Diver and his sister Pearl to learn to read, and she had no intentions of mating with me, they'd warily agreed.

Many other females had done the same. We'd been forced to extend our classes into other rooms. I still taught basic reading, Algier had a growing class, as did Lara, and Tomura had taken over the more advanced readers. Rowena, with Mitzy's help, taught history. Or at least, what we knew of it. There still were many things both about the humans and our world we didn't know. I kept hoping to find more information, yet the books were oddly silent about our snow covered planet.

Rowena's warning growl alerted me to possible danger. Quickly I got to my paws, my eyes following the progress of a strange white wolf with brown feet and a blotchy matching tip on its tail. Also, I saw a small snow colored feline riding on the back of, surly I couldn't be seeing…I'd heard stories…there before me where two Spotted Ghosts!

Chapter 14

His first view of the building didn't impress him, dull red bricks, windows, a door that looked like it was always open. Carefully he adjusted his position so he wouldn't fall off the back of the larger feline. At least the creature hadn't lost the precious book he'd found. He couldn't wait to continue reading his exciting discovery.

The final days of the journey had been very difficult. It had snowed and snowed. When they'd finally emerged from under the heavily bogged limbs, the deep drifts had made traveling slow. They'd found a dead deer, ate, and kept going.

Of course, there had been that very amusing incident with the bison. The big lumbering creatures really hadn't been interested in them, but the bull had pawed the ground and charged them, warning off three potential predators.

More taking shelter in old human dwellings. Houses, he corrected himself. Eating more deer, sometimes a rabbit, and their group constantly traveling down the mountain until they emerged into the valley. Once they'd arrived in the ruin dotted expanse, the wolf had found more its kind and he assumed they'd been directed here.

The canine trotted up the hill. Another wolf met it, showing its teeth. Others like him and about his size floundered in the snow, taking refuge around their mothers. A very large feline, cat the humans had once called them, stood next to the wolves. Somehow he sensed that one was the dominant male.

They joined the wolf. He jumped down blinking at the dominant male, then noticed the gray female on the steps. Round green eyes met his blue ones. She turned away and pretended not to have seen him.

Some sort of agreement must have been reached and they were allowed to enter. He didn't really like the darkened hall. The other cats scampered down it and into various rooms. Curious, he peaked into one seeing rolled up fabric. In others there were books laying on the floor and kittens gathering around the pages.

Excited now, he forgot about his traveling companions and bounded in to join a group. They moved, allowing him to read the page. One of the larger cats walked in. The kittens ignored him and he kept reading.

~ * ~

"He'll be fine," I told the new wolf, Dermot. Rowena translated since the dialect varied from what I had learned from the packs. She seemed to understand him better.

She listened to his reply and said, "Snow Fur can't hear."

Surprised I glanced in the room. The other kittens listened raptly to Lara while Snow Fur kept reading. I wondered what male had allowed a defective kitten to survive.

"Where did he learn to read?"

"He says the cubs told him Snow Fur learned on his own."

"What is that the male ghost has?"

"Something Snow Fur wouldn't leave behind."

We entered the library and the male, Valmiki I'd been told, put the brown thing down. Deciding to find out more about it later, I turned my attention back to the wolf. "Ask him how he ended up with a feline and two Spotted Ghosts."

After hearing his story, I couldn't believe it! Not only were we and the wolves intelligent, but so were the Ghosts! I began to wonder if any other creatures were as well.

Also, I worried about the two legs. If they had been into the mountains and I knew they'd gone off in the vast plains, I wondered where else they might go? Would they return to explore our valley and discover our new community? And, if they had killed a wolf, what would they do to us?

"Rowena, when the packs return, tell them what Dermot told us. I'm going to have Cleopatra tell the other females." Cleo, and the other females whose kittens we taught, had moved into the houses around the school. Most lived in growing groups like my wives and I, although the males stayed away. "We need to watch for the two legs and come up with a plan to defend ourselves."

"I agree. When the packs return, perhaps you should meet with the dominants."

"Do you think any of the packs will accept Dermot?" I knew a pack would accept a wolf they still considered a puppy, but I wasn't sure about a grown male.

"No. But he can den with me."

The two ghosts wrestled, knocking over a few books on the higher shelves. They quickly dodged the falling volumes to keep from being hit. Dermot growled at them, and they stopped their play fighting.

Now what was I going to do with them?

~ * ~

He knew he'd missed something important. The other kittens bumped each other and the female looked directly at him. Cocking his head to the side, he could only stare back Finally, she ignored him and after a while they all left. He read longer and later set off in search of his travel companions.

He finally found the large library and his special book lying on the floor. Pushing it to a corner, he opened the pages, some of which were ripped and began to read.

It's been snowing for several days and Daddy finally gave up trying to get a bus to pick us up. He loaded up my grandfather's old SUV with blankets, food and water. Daddy even went up to the attic and pulled down all the camping gear.

I sat by the fire and watched the big flakes out the window. My sister and her husband had been one of the last people to get passage on one of the ships. The military came and escorted them away. Mommy cried and begged daddy for us all to go with them. He said No Way were we going to leave the place he called home.

Ships? He'd have to find out about those. There had to be books here that would tell him.

Daddy also said he thinks it will be warmer farther south. Mommy packed a few keepsakes and we got into the big noisy SUV. It was very crowded and I had to find a snuggly spot for myself on all the stuff.

There were a few blank pages. He nosed through to the next entry.

I don't know why Daddy didn't use one of the highways on our side of the mountain. For some reason he chose to go over the summit and now we're stuck in this old rundown log cabin.

The SUV ran out of gas and there wasn't any in the old pumps. Daddy got all mad and hit the antiques and swore, and stomped around a lot. Mommy just sat and cried. We finally found this place and Daddy made a nice fire.

Fire to keep warm instead of curling up together or on a warm fur. Now there was an idea!

Mommy made me hot chocolate and used the last of the marshmallows. She also heated up soup in a big kettle and tried to make biscuits. They ended up all lumpy and sticky. We ate our dinner and when we were done, Mommy and Daddy went upstairs to talk in one of the bedrooms.

More pages were blank. One of them had odd blotches.

Daddy went outside last night and didn't come back. Mommy keeps saying he will, but I don't think so. We also lost the old radio we used to listen for any type of news. Mommy says she thinks the batteries died. I think the stations are off the air.

Almost all our food is gone. I really miss hot chocolate. Best we can do is melt snow and drink it with some sugar. At least it's warm.

Mommy isn't really good with the fire. She feeds it more wood, yet it keeps flickering, like it wants to go out and die. If it does, we'll die too.

I remember in school the teacher talking about how cold it is at the poles. About how the Eskimos make igloos and live off seal blubber and have funny sleds they travel on. Wish we had a sled so we could leave this awful cabin.

The next page had funny shapes all over it. He had no idea what they were supposed to be.

It's dark now. Mommy is asleep on the couch, all snug and cozy in her sleeping bag. I can't sleep. My nose is cold, and I can't feel my toes. My tummy hurts and I'm hungry.

Our fire doesn't keep the room warm anymore. Thick ice covers all the windows. I think the door is frozen shut or maybe the snow is so high we'll never be able to get out.

There were more blank pages. He flipped ahead to where more words were.

My sister talked about God a lot. About how good and loving He is. What kind of god would allow such a horrible thing to happen? Why would He kill so many people?

Why do I have to die?

Death was a part of his world. He stared at the words puzzled. Had the humans lived so isolated from everything they didn't understand to die was just part of life?

The pretty gray cat walked past him and jumped up on a chair. She groomed herself and curled into ball. He had no doubt she was asleep, although he would like to find a way to communicate with her. He'd have to discover a way.

Returning his attention to his book, he read on.

Some bad men broke into the cabin. They took Mommy upstairs. When they came back down they took our sleeping bags and cooking stuff and yelled a lot about why didn't we have any food or was I such a mean kid I'd hidden it?

I cried and they finally left me alone. I crept upstairs. Mommy was on one of the beds. She was dead. I could tell 'cuz there was blood everywhere and her eyes were open and she wasn't moving. It smelled awful like something sweet mixed with cleaning stuff Mommy used in the bathrooms.

Scared I screamed and screamed and when I stopped I cried for a long time.

He understood about losing a mother. He'd lost two. The one whom he'd been born to and the one who had adopted and partially raised him.

I'm all alone. I'm trying to keep the fire going, but I'm so hungry! All I have is snow and it's cold. The bad men even took our cups.

I shut the door where my dead Mommy lies. I did find some blankets in a closet and I wrapped up in them. Not enough though. I'm shaking I'm so cold!

I keep wishing Daddy had listened to Mommy and we'd left on one of the ships. I'd be someplace warm with lots of food.

More blank pages, a couple had lines moving in patterns.

I decided I can't stay here anymore. Maybe someplace in the town there are other people. Even if there aren't it doesn't matter. Maybe I'll find some food.

I'm gonna hide my diary behind a loose brick I found on the fireplace. Maybe someone will find it someday. When all the snow and cold goes away.

But the scientists said it'll be a long time.

In bold letters the diary ended.

MANDY JENKINS

~ * ~

Snow Fur showed me his book. I read through the entries. Too bad the child, the writer, had not gone into detail about what exactly had happened according to the scientists.

The early pages were filled with things that happened at her school, about her sister getting married and how her Daddy was thinking about transferring up to another part of the state, whatever that meant, to do some special work.

I had no doubt the child had died. One so young could not have survived without help and there didn't seem to be any for her. Her plight made me sad. I returned the book to Snow Fur who found a shelf for it to sit on. He found another book and I left him reading, wishing there was some way to talk with this astounding deaf kitten!

Algier returned at sunset with his new mate. She stood shyly behind him. Starlite rushed forward to touch her nose to her brother's. She went around him and addressed the new female.

"Welcome."

The young female hesitantly stepped forward. Algier had chosen a lovely tabby. She held her dark brown head high. Her graceful movements accented her irregular tawny stripes. She kept her chest a pristine white and her feet where black.

"My name is Sheba."

"And I am Starlite."

"I'm Tomura," my Siamese wife greeted. "We took fabric scrapes to the gym so you could make a warm nest for your new kittens."

"Thank you."

"Algier," I said, "I need to speak to you."

He joined me and I told him about the new wolf Dermot, the deaf kitten and the two Snow Ghosts.

"You seem to be known even far away," he observed absently, as if it didn't matter to him.

"I never thought to be."

"You're the first of us to learn to read. You'll be remembered by your kitten's kittens, and their kittens. Probably, as the humans used to say, 'You'll go down in history.'"

I didn't know if I would be comfortable with that thought.

"I see your females, I mean wives, are showing mine to her new home."

"Are you still going to want Sasha?" I couldn't help myself. I had to know if a challenge was coming.

He blinked his blue eyes at me. "Perhaps."

~ * ~

The library was a wonderful place. He'd found so many interesting books and liked the many ideas presented in them. In fact, he decided he should have a name. Now, he was certain his mother and his adopted one had surely called him something, but since he had no way to find out what it was, he named himself.

He chose the name Mute. It wasn't fancy or anything. Simple and appropriate and he liked it.

Also, he noticed most of the other kittens avoided him, except the gray tabby. She seemed to want to be around him and he began to share some of his discoveries with her.

Like the article he had just found. He'd been exploring under the bookcases and found a magazine. Pulling it out, one of the titles on the cover caught his attention. Curious whether it might contain more information about the terrible thing that had happened in Mandy's writings, he nosed through the pages to the article.

Unfortunately, a lot of it had been torn away. He did garner some information. The pretty female crept close to him, still trying to make it seem like she was disinterested. He knew she peered over his shoulder.

To help prepare for this national emergency President Howard has traveled to the Arctic to confer with the Inuit and plans to return with survival techniques for families. The estimated time for his trip will be three weeks and his findings will be printed as soon as they are available.

He wondered if the findings had ever been printed. By the number of bones they'd found in various houses, somehow he doubted it. Most seemed to have died trying to keep warm or maybe they had starved as it seemed Mandy had.

There wasn't much else in the article. Just estimates about temperatures, and how much damage it would do to crops, and suggestions people start thinking about either taking ships or else migrating toward the equator. He pushed it away.

Tactfully Mute walked in an arc around the female. Gathering his hindquarters under him for a long leap, he jumped up on the counter. Many items littered the glossy surface. He recognized a holder and a pencil, which some other kitten must have been playing with. It had teeth marks all over it.

The large item near the end interested him. Like the mirror in one of their shelters it reflected his image. In front was a large board with mixed up letters, one small side section contained numbers.

Interesting. He'd read in some of the magazines about something called a computer. The humans had used them for all sorts of things. Keeping finances and talking with each other. Reaching out a paw he stepped on one of the letters. It gave under his weight.

He tried another. The same. An idea began to form in his mind. He needed to do some more research. He reasoned there had to be more information here somewhere, that could him figure out how the computer worked. *If* it could be powered up…

The idea stuck in his mind. Before dawn he was up searching the various books in the library. He found several on computers stacked in a corner. Studying the pages he despaired. His one question was *how* did one turn on the computer? Most simply instructed to turn it on and do this or that.

He sat in front of the computer trying to decipher its mysteries. A button with an odd symbol on it *not* covered in the book caught his eye. Pushing it, he jumped back when the screen lit up, darkened with odd letters in strange orders changing several times before settling into a steady pattern.

Recognizing the screen from his reading he hurriedly leaped down to examine one of the books open on the floor. Quickly checking the directions he resumed his place and moved his paw along the small rectangle at the bottom of the key board. A little arrow appeared. He found what he wanted and after a couple of attempts, managed to open the program.

Mute looked hard at the board and pushed a letter. It appeared on the screen. He tried again. More letters. He practiced closing and reopening the program. Finally he typed.

MY NAME IS MUTE.

Chapter 15

Lavena and Herne greeted me and sat down on their haunches. Her daughters arrived soon after with their mates. I'd chosen Tomura's room since Snow Fur had books scattered all over the library floor.

"We've all listened to Dermot and know what happened in the mountains."

Yseult interrupted me with a sharp yip. "The two legs here didn't kill one of the pack."

"But I lost a pup," Lavena reminded us.

"We don't know if the two legs killed the pup," her new mate gently responded.

"They took it."

I wondered how I would have responded if one of my kittens had been taken. Would I have come out of hiding and fought the invaders?

"Dermot doesn't know for certain the two legs killed his brother." Phelan scratched at his ear.

"The tracks seemed to indicate they had." Dermot had been very sure about the cause of his brother's death. From some of the early accounts I'd read, if the two legs were humans, I had no problem believing they would kill a wolf. "We have to decide, beyond banding together, what we are going to do to protect ourselves."

"Maybe we could lead them away," Lavena suggested.

"If there are only a few of them," Phelan said. "We could kill them."

"And if more come?" his mate Cara asked.

~ * ~

The pretty gray female joined him on the counter. She cocked her head, like he'd seen the dominant male do many times, as she read the message he'd typed. He added. WHAT'S YOUR NAME?

She'd watched as he typed. Almost hesitantly she copied his motions, taking longer since she didn't know where the letters were.

SASHA.

ARE YOU A KITTEN OF THE DOMINANT MALE?

YOU MEAN WORD WARRIOR? She responded. HE FOUND

ME. She went on to tell him her entire story. When she finished she told him, THE WOLF, DERMOT, SAYS YOUR NAME IS SNOW FUR.

Maybe the name did fit. I PREFER MUTE.

I'LL CALL YOU THAT.

Back and forth they typed, him learning about the new home he'd come to and about some of the stories the wolf and the Spotted Ghosts, as she called them, had told the community.

MANY OTHER FEMALES LIVE IN THE HOUSES AROUND US.

I'D SEEN OTHERS AND WONDERED.

He stopped when other kittens entered the room. Sasha jumped down and pretended disinterest. The others gathered around an open book and Mute covertly continued using the program.

~ * ~

Jojo retrieved the book off the shelf as Nan skittered around her brothers and sisters. He noticed the new white male playing with the odd counter thing, but ignored him. He and Nan had other things to do.

Together they settled in the farthest corner on the edge of the fraying rug. Gently he nosed the brittle pages open hoping it was the same place they'd stopped reading.

"I think we were here." Nan turned a couple more pages. "The human was about to go against the giant."

"What's a giant?"

"Remember the story about the boy and his plant and the giant?"

The young wolf had an itch and scratched his shoulder with his large paw. If nothing more, it let him try to recall what Nan was talking about.

"Oh, wait, you might not. I think you were napping." Nan quickly told him the story. Not that it really helped him understand what a giant was.

"A very big human?" It was the closest he came to understanding.

"That's right!" Nan licked his muzzle. "Now," she moved so she half laid on his front paw. "Let's keep reading and find out what happens."

~ * ~

We didn't come up with a plan. The wolves distrusted the new male although they had no trouble believing the two legs would kill them if given the opportunity. They left, arguing about what to do. I decided to rejoin my kittens and wives. A part of me wondered what the wolves' reaction had been to Rowena offering a place in her den to Dermot.

I rejoined my wives as we entered the library. My kittens were scattered over the room doing everything from hiding behind bookshelves using them as cover in mock hunting games seeking prey, to wrestling each other practicing their battle skills. Some were reading an open book, while others washed themselves in preparation for a nap. Nan and Jojo were in the corner reading The Provider's words. I wondered if they'd come to believe in Him as I now did.

Carefully I moved around the many books on the floor. Above me on the counter Snow Fur intently concentrated on the mirror thing which now glared almost blindingly. I jumped up to discover what he was doing.

A faint movement caught my attention and I discovered Sasha beside him. "Mute knows how to write," she informed me.

"Who knows how to do what?" I blinked and stared at her.

"We've been talking on that." She moved her head to indicate the mirror thing.

Excited one of us could write, I wished Snow Fur, had she called him Mute? Could hear me and teach my kittens. A new skill shouldn't be lost to us. Perhaps Sasha could have him teach her, or maybe he already had since she said they'd been talking on it.

He kept moving his paw around and I moved closer to observe what he was doing. A small rectangle thing, a shape Algier had taught me, sat below the odd board thing. My eyes traveled to the mirror where another shape, an arrow I think, moved about. I had to resist a strong temptation to chase it.

"Sasha," I spoke to my daughter, "I want you to ask Snow Fur,"

"His name is Mute," she corrected me.

"Mute," I conceded, "to teach you more about writing."

"I've done some already," she said. "On this com…puter."

Computer? I'd always been curious what that word had meant. I observed how Mute was using it and how Sasha copied the movements. "When you're ready," I told my daughter, "start teaching your brothers and sisters."

She blinked green eyes at me. I had no idea if she would obey or not.

Mute hopped back. Both of us turned to see why. The mirror had produced a long list of things I'd never heard of, like save, save as, and others just as mysterious. The younger male blinked and pressed keys before I could stop him. Had he done something wise? I placed my paw on his to gain his attention.

"Let him be, Word Warrior," Sasha softly scolded, sitting beside him. "I've wondered about this computer, haven't you?"

Of course I had.

"I'll watch him and learn."

I hesitated and knew I had to agree with her. No doubt my daughter would be an excellent student. Also, I hoped this device would not be a threat to us. I had not forgotten when it made a screeching noise.

~ * ~

Vaguely Mute sensed the tension behind him which eased when the male, what had Sasha called him? Oh yes, Word Warrior, had left. He had no idea why the sudden list had bothered the other. Mute sat considering all the options he'd already learned in the books that he'd studied. Finally, he chose one.

Mute knew it was now safe to close the program and figured out if the button that had turned it on, it probably also shut it off. The screen darkened like he'd first discovered it. Sasha licked his face and jumped down to the floor waiting for him to join her.

They went outside to discover part of the wolves' kill waiting. The other cats tore bits of meat off and found private places to eat. He chose some for himself and took a spot next to Jyotis, Sasha had told him the name of the Ghosts, and ate. When he finished, the female used her tongue to clean him and he fell asleep next to her familiar vibrating side.

~ * ~

I'd almost forgotten about the Spotted Ghosts. Dermot kept them away from us and with him and Rowena. The female enjoyed his company and I began to wonder if the two of them might mate and form their own pack.

Lazily I sprawled outside watching the sun slide behind the sharp silhouetted mountains marking the darkening sky with red, blue and orange. Heavy clouds rolled slowly over them and the scent of another storm teasingly touched my nose.

"We'll have another storm," Tomura observed as she sat beside me.

"I yearn for green and growing things like I see in the books," I confided.

"It would be nice to see leaves on the trees and colorful flowers."

"Jungles for us to hide in and hunt prey." I knew I must sound wistful.

"Insects to chase and small plentiful rodents." She licked a spot on my ear.

"The books I read say it was once different." I cleaned my paw and pulled at a loosening nail. "Yet, still, the records we read are vague on what happened."

My wife was silent briefly. "Perhaps," she paused. "There wasn't time to write down what happened."

"The book Mute has,"

"Who's Mute?"

"We call him Snow Fur. Sasha told me he has chosen another name for himself."

"How?"

I hadn't shared this about him. "He knows how to write. The mirror thing, a computer, is the way he used to talk to us." I stretched long and rolled. "The book he has is by a human and talks about some of what happened."

"Oh, that book." She twitched her tail. "I read it. The human simply called it 'The Terrible Thing'."

Tomura had read it? That surprised me. "There has to be more writings." Frustration welled in me.

"I'm sure as we discover more libraries and books we'll find more information." She blinked. "I think I will ask Cleo to ask the other females to search the houses they're in."

I hadn't thought of that. Perhaps there were more records we hadn't found and written by those who had once inhabited the houses. I knew too, I would have to start searching libraries farther away, like the one we'd taken refuge in with Algier. Somehow, I would have to convince the wolves to help us again.

"My kittens are sleeping in Callie's room tonight," Tomura told me. "Would you like to share my nest?"

Cold wind heralding the coming storm ruffled my fur with long deep claws. Sharing warmth with my wife would be welcome. "Yes."

She rose regally and I followed her to her room.

~ * ~

Mute dodged quickly when the very dusty book dropped to the shredded rug. Excitedly he pounced on the thick pages. He and Sasha had been exploring some of the upper shelves. They'd found this one and he'd pushed it near the edge intending to have Sasha shove it over after he'd gotten down. It had fallen accidentally when he'd jumped.

Sasha joined him. Together they opened the pages. Inside the thick binding were many scriggly lines, much like his special book written by Mandy. Not sure if he was disappointed or thrilled by what he'd found, he nosed the musty paper.

His eyes examined the words. Sasha sneezed and he felt her breath on his face. He shyly licked her muzzle and together, they began to read.

When it first happened, people ran into the streets screaming hysterically. Police had a difficult time trying to stop the looting. Rocks were thrown through the store windows. The first targets were the home improvement stores. In the riots everything from wood, heavily insulated windows, Porte potties, draperies, rugs, and anything else that might be useful were taken.

Grocery store shelves were emptied. The first things gone were bottled water, canned and packaged goods, any type of food that wouldn't spoil or need to be cooked. Most in the more populated areas were the first to lose power.

Sporting goods like hiking boots, heavy down coats, sleeping bags, and even guns were in high demand. Blankets, mattresses or anything else that could be useful and help a person to survive.

The holocasts continued for awhile. Scientists speculated on the length and tried to reassure the populace they would survive. After all, something similar had happened before during the Middle Ages and humanity had continued. The horrible result was that many people foolishly believed them and never left their homes. They either froze or died of starvation.

It was unbelievable.

Explained the many bones he'd seen. Gullible people. They should have at least moved to a warmer place. Where ever that might be.

The last ship to leave did so under heavy guard. Masses of people rushed the port trying to get on board. The holocasts were bloody and even the reporter assigned to the story said she wished she'd been smart enough to book passage for herself and her family.

He really did need to find out what ships were. There had to be a book here somewhere that explained them.

Many people didn't make it out of the states. Fuel ran out. Some tried to make fires but even then, there simply wasn't enough for the demand. Others tried to chop down trees. I hate to think of how many died because they didn't know what they were doing and the massive trunks, I don't even want to think about it.

The fire part reminded him of what had happened to Mandy.

Many were so hungry they hunted and killed the dogs. And when they could catch them, the cats. Some even hunted coyotes, foxes and rabbits.

Eat a cat? Mute huffed in disgust. He turned to see Sasha's reaction. Her tail jerked angrily back and forth.

Rumors drifted about elephants, caribou, buffalo, cheetahs, tigers, and lions, loose in the streets. Perhaps one of the keepers at the zoo had taken pity on the poor animals and released them. Not that most would have survived anyway. Between the intense cold and people hunting them, they no doubt perished before reaching warmer climates.

Too, how many people died trying to hunt beasts who could out run or out fight them? There was a report, more of a rumor really, about a man trampled by an elephant.

Mute had read about elephants. Even he'd been squashed under one of its feet.

Blank pages. He turned many more before he found writing again. Squinting he wondered if his eyes deceived him. The scriggles were different and not as clear.

The teacher who wrote this earlier is dead. Didn't know I'd also hidden here and I saw where this book was kept.

Mute wondered who this new writer was.

Faint paw prints had been imprinted on the page. He lifted his paw and measured the size with his own. They were much larger. He continued reading.

I watch the cat females here. There is one who makes her home in the old firehouse. She found a warm coat and placed her kittens in the large pockets. Many times I've seen her hunting, dodging us humans, dragging rabbits and whatever small rodents she can find back to her den.

As for the others, they continue to raid the stores for whatever supplies they can find, which aren't many. Some are still living in small groups, while others prefer to live alone, like me. I've seen them hang blankets over the windows and doors trying to keep the cold out. Even burn wood or books or who knows what, in ancient gas fireplaces, stupid useless invention all in the name of environmentalism. Despite everything, many are dead.

He turned the page.

I found a poem today and decided it should be in the book. Maybe one day someone will read it and know that we humans weren't just a bunch of stupid animals.

The rest of the page was blank. Turning to the next, Mute found a sheet tucked in. At least it hadn't fallen out. Sasha leaned closer to see what he'd found. Carefully he nosed it open and they read it together.

QUESTIONS
Darkness.
Wasn't the Earth dark
in the beginning?

Didn't God
put
a sun in the sky?

Why is it so dark now?
Where is the once blue sky?
How came this cloudy and snow filled world?

What will
become
of the human race?

Has God abandoned
His Creation?
Darkness.

A few pages later the unknown writer had added more.

Well, we might ask what will become of our world. We'd been warned. Many times. Yet because such an event was just a historical note, we foolishly ignored it. Now, it's too late.

Since I must stay, I'll record what I can. There needs to be some sort record.

The entries stopped. Mute cocked his head to one side puzzled. Stashed under the back cover were articles, magazines, and other things.

Sasha tugged at his neck with her sharp teeth. No doubt she wanted to do something else. He wanted to ignore her and read more of this discovery. But since she seemed to have tired of reading he decided to come back later. He pushed the book closer to the counter near the computer.

When he finished, Mute pounced on Sasha and the two began a game

of chasing each other. When she finally quit she curled into a tight ball
on the chair. Making sure she slept, he pulled out the magazines hoping
to discover more.

~ * ~

I'd noticed Mute rarely came out of the library. The fact Sasha
preferred to stay with him I'd also noted. She still hadn't come into heat
and I wondered about that as well.

Sniffing the breeze I debated about hunting. I detected no storm scent.
The sun began to rise reflecting dark pink off the stringy clouds, hovering
over the snow covered mountains.

Odd. I had not thought of trying to discover the name of the
ancient human city where we lived. No doubt there were records.
Somewhere.

"Word Warrior," Starlite's soft voice called to me. She came to stand
beside me glancing up to also enjoy the sunrise. The bell from her mother
tinkled and I wondered how she'd managed to secure it around her neck.
Noticing my gaze she said, "My kittens kept playing with it. I was afraid
they'd lose it."

Curious as to why her mother might have left the bell I asked, "Does
Callie know anything else about your mother?"

"No. She told Algier and I all she knew. Are you hunting today?"

I sniffed again. "I haven't decided yet."

"Perhaps you should take some of the kittens with you."

Starlite's suggestion was a good idea. The younger males were old
enough for their first distance hunt. I followed my mate back inside. She
took me to Callie's small room where our Elder had all the kittens
gathered around her. I guessed she was telling them stories again.

Callie lifted her orange head and glared at me. "You interrupted."

"My apologies." I had no real need to placate her. "I've come to take
the males on their first distance hunt."

Many heads popped up.

"Really, Daddy?" Clomper blinked his green eyes.

"Really."

Nine separated themselves from their sisters and followed me outside.
Pausing at the door I considered which direction to go. Leading my
kittens down the hill we headed toward the coldest wind. I heard a bark
behind me. Rowena bounded up with one of the Spotted Ghosts.

"Which one?" I inquired.

"Valmiki," she answered as she, and the ghost, joined the hunting party.

Passing collapsed houses and skeleton trees, I again found myself longing for the seasons described in the books. How nice it would be to roll in grass and be able to hide behind leafy bushes.

"How many sunrises will we be gone, Daddy?" Neutron trotted beside me.

"Many." In the back of my mind I was considering exploring some of the buildings. Perhaps we'd find more books and answers to my many questions.

"What are we going to hunt?" Chev wanted to know.

"Whatever we find."

Heading in the direction of the mountains we climbed an incline and moved behind an old store. White spread out before us, broken only by the remnants of the humans' past. The sun rose higher and we trotted on.

Dashing in front of me some of my kittens rolled in the snow and others teased each other in mock fights. An unaware rabbit darted out and several chased it until it escaped down a hole. It was good training for a real hunt.

Chapter 16

The first sunset we stayed in a store. Bare silver metal stripped of whatever it had once held towered above us. Still, they'd make good, safe beds for us to sleep on and Rowena dragged bits of rug to make them warmer.

Valmiki killed several rats and shared his meager hunt with us. We gulped down fresh meat and drank cold water from bowl things in small rooms. The Ghost stretched out and several of my kittens tentatively approached him. He licked Maurie's black spotted head and my son took it as an invitation. He snuggled against the large feline and several of his brothers joined them.

Rowena took a place beside me. Trotsky, Sterling, and Hardy joined us. We huddled together through the dark.

~ * ~

Jyotis brought Mute a nice fat rat to eat and he shared his feast with her and Sasha. He wondered where the larger male was and he typed that out on the computer. Sasha explained Word Warrior had taken all the males on a distance hunt and that Valmiki, and Rowena, one of the wolves, had gone with them

Mute began exploring some of the other rooms looking for more books. The many writings he'd found made him more and more curious. The time before the Long Winter had been different and he really wanted to find out what exactly had happened.

The magazines in back of the book had only contained articles on how to survive and not gone into any details about the actual event itself. The general advice had been either to flee or else try to survive the severe cold.

He paused at the door of one room. The strong odor of wolf, which he knew so well from his long trip with Dermot, attacked his nose. Slowly he backed away and chose another to explore.

Nearby a door sat slightly ajar. He managed to squeeze his small frame through. He allowed his eyes to adjust and the first thing he noticed was that the room had no windows. A dark couch sat along one wall and several overturned chairs and a couple of shattered tables were scattered on the floor. There were no paw prints in the dust so no other creature had been in here.

He jumped up on the couch and sneezed as a cloud of dust erupted. An old phone sat on one end. Odd. From the articles he'd read there had been things called holovids. Humans had used them for communication. At the other end were several papers. Mute hopped over and tried to sort through them. Each seemed to have different scriggles on them. He finally found one to read.

I told my class to write how they felt about what the scientists say is going to happen and how their families were getting ready for it. Some of what they wrote shocked me. Many of the parents have refused to believe it and have made no plans to evacuate.

My heart breaks for these children. They won't survive. How I wish the law would allow me to take them all away to a safe place.

As for me, I have somewhere to go. My sister and her family are military. She got clearance for me to join them in the mountain. They have supplies and advancements, though she spoke of this in a hushed voice. I knew they were never going to be shared with the general public.

I remember all the stories I read in college from the personal accounts of those who lived through horrible events like the holocaust, or escaped from war torn countries. In my mind I had a hard time digesting the awful events they described, despite the finding of grisly remains centuries later.

Will those many generations from now, view our civilization that way?

The writing ended. Mute shoved it aside to read the next.

~ * ~

Loud screeching noises started me of my out sleep. Rowena growled and Valmiki snarled. My kittens stood still in terror. I crawled on my belly to the large windows and surveyed the world outside, still bathed in near darkness.

Snow whipped in the air like a storm. A metal monster with whirling wings similar to a flapper plowed its long feet into the drifts. The side opened and several two legs dropped out.

"Hide!" I ordered as I watched the two legs in bright orange approach the building. The sounds of soft scratches behind me told me my kittens were obeying. I wiggled around so I was hidden in the shadow of some stacked boxes.

Harsh sounds which I assumed was their way of communicating

with each other echoed. Hunkering down, I observed them. A thin light bobbed through the building.

They stood near the entrance gesturing at each other. Finally, they left. The monster screamed back into the air.

I stayed where I was until the cold reached the skin below my fur. When it seemed the two legs would not return, I knew it was safe to come out of hiding. "They've gone. Come out."

Patters of clawed feet and faint clicking from all over. I returned to the back of the store. We huddled together for warmth. My kittens dropped off into sleep, but I stayed awake and kept watch. Rowena joined me in my vigil.

~ * ~

Mute returned from his explorations and sat in front of the computer again. The new papers he'd found didn't tell him anything he hadn't already read. Most were from children who had been scared and worried about what would happen to their pets and if it meant they couldn't have any more new toys.

So close and yet still no more information. He'd just have to keep searching. The truth had to be out there somewhere.

He jumped down and found Sasha waiting for him. She rubbed against him and he joined her when she leaped to the window to stare outside. Fat flakes fell and the sky had turned an ugly gray.

Mute curled up with Sasha, her head resting on his side. He felt her body rumbling and was soothed by the vibrations. Content, he closed his blue eyes to nap.

~ * ~

The storm was not a welcome sight at sunrise. I stared outside as the sky grew even darker and winds blew so hard they obscured the broken buildings beyond the large clear space.

Rowena sat beside me. "What now?"

"We wait."

"Valmiki found more rats in one of the rooms. He is feeding the kittens."

At least they wouldn't be hungry and complaining about it all day. That was good. Maybe we'd explore this massive building and make a game out of it to keep them amused. We joined them and I ate. A couple of kittens scampered behind a long counter to relieve themselves.

When they came back we began to explore. Many metal shelves

hovered above us. One held an object and Poppin scrambled up and poked his brown head inside. He backed up and sneezed loudly.

"Just big and empty," he complained.

We moved on. Poppin found another object leaning against the wall. He bumped it and it fell with a loud splat. Spinning around, his fur stood straight up and he hissed at the offensive thing. When it made no aggressive move, my kitten cautiously approached and sniffed it.

"Smells sort of like the dead trees," he informed me.

Near the back we found a curious section. Small balls littered the floor. My kittens jumped on them and soon were batting them with their paws, rolling them under cracks and flopping down, trying to get them out. I sat watching, glad we'd found something to amuse them.

Valmiki sat next to Rowena. His great yellow eyes slowly blinked and he lowered himself to the cold floor, placing his head on his large paws. His tail twitched.

"Does he want to play as well?" I asked Rowena.

The wolf glanced at the larger feline and spoke haltingly to the Ghost. She had to listen intently for the answer. Dermot must be teaching her because I had no idea she could speak to the Ghosts.

"He doesn't want to harm any of your kittens," she told me.

"Valmiki could still play with one of the balls."

"He's used to wrestling with his sister. Doesn't like to play alone."

Hardy's solid black body bounded up. "I'll play with him." He pounced on Valmiki.

The larger feline hesitated before whole heartedly joining in a game of chase. Their antics attracted the attention of my other kittens. Before long they were all running after each other, hiding on shelves or behind tall objects, darting out and fleeing again. When they tired, they piled on top of each other, and Valmiki, and took a long nap.

While they napped I went back to the windows. More snow piled up and drifted into deep banks. The wind blew even harder, rattling the half open doors. Cold crept in. Shivering I retreated to the back. It would be better if we slept here.

Rowena had found some cushions. She dragged them behind one of the shelf units to help block the cold which crept in like a stalking feline. Together we nudged the Ghost and kittens awake and moved them to the warmer spot.

We curled up with them as the building creaked. I closed my eyes, keeping part of my mind alert as I rested. Mattie shifted from on top of Valmiki and crawled to my side. His brown and black body, so like me, shivered.

"I'm cold, Daddy."

I made a space between Rowena and I. Mattie laid against my long fur. The wolf whined and moved enough so my kitten touched both of us. Soon, Mattie stopped shaking and fell into an exhausted sleep.

Shifting to get more comfortable on the lumpy cushion, I continued to listen to the building. Something rattled overhead, cracked loudly, smacked against the roof several times and stopped.

Rowena's head popped up. She growled low in her throat, alerting me to possible danger.

From the front a loud roar came followed by busting glass. The building shook. We all scrambled to our paws, my kittens scattering in several directions. I heard Rowena bark several times and I saw Valmiki run after my sons trying to get them all together and bring them back to me.

I ran to the front of the building, afraid we might be trapped. Snow blew inside and I pushed against the chilly claws. Outside, many body lengths away, bright orange and yellow flames twirled and black acrid smoke bit my nose. I stopped, surprised the building hadn't trapped us. The large windows were gone, the shattered glass pieces fast being covered by snow.

Twitching my tail in agitation I pondered what to do. Did I dare lead my young out into the storm? Or should we stay here and hope the fire didn't consume the store as well? Bright flares swirled upward carrying glowing danger.

"Fire bad," Rowena half growled and whined.

"So is the storm."

Her large white head jerked up as a wailing howl echoed. Before I could stop her she sprang out and circled the blaze. She yipped and howled with a mixture of encouragement and desperation. From somewhere in the fire she was answered. I watched amazed as a half-grown wolf crawled through the tangled mess.

The two struggled back toward us. Valmiki leaped out to help, supporting the younger wolf as it staggered. My young gathered around me all of them asking what happened and what was going on. The three reached us and the injured wolf collapsed.

Valmiki voiced a sound that was familiar and yet not. Rowena translated. "He says we need a healer."

I remembered Lavena had helped Callie once and spoke my thought.

"No." Lavena nudged the other wolf. "We have some knowledge. Not about this. Cub hurt very bad."

Wrinkling my nose I almost gagged. The stench of burnt fur and flesh was overwhelming.

The Ghost said something to Rowena before he sprinted off into the storm. She watched him go and said, "He goes to Dermot."

How could Dermot help us?

"Dermot knows where a Spotted Ghost healer dens."

I remembered Dermot speaking about the healer when he told us his story. The younger wolf began to whine in pain and writhe around on the cold floor.

"Snow," Neutron announced bouncing out and returning with a mouth full. He dumped it on a burned patch of hindquarters. "All of you," he ordered his brothers, "help."

My kittens hurried to comply. After a time the wolf quieted though his brown eyes reflected the great pain he was in. Perhaps it would have been more merciful to allow him to die in the fire, which was now slowly dying down leaving behind a molten mass.

"How did you know what to do?" I asked my son.

"Read it in a medical book," Neutron proudly replied. "We need to keep the wolf warm."

"There were cushions in the back, but how did we get the wolf there?"

"What's its name?" Neutron asked Rowena.

She inquired and got a tired pain filled answer. "Says his name is Iden."

The cub began to shiver. Gently Rowena urged him to his feet and he painfully wobbled to the back of the store. Neutron walked beside Iden gently encouraging the young wolf. When we reached the cushions we settled the cub and my kittens scrambled all round him to try and keep him warm.

As the storm howled loudly as a wolf pack, we waited.

~ * ~

Nan roused from her sleep with a sense of something was very wrong. Jojo whined beside her and she knew he felt it, too.

"We should ask The Provider to protect my Daddy and my brothers."

"More than that wrong."

"I know, but we don't know what."

Her friend agreed and together they prayed before they both sensed they could go back to sleep. Nan closed her eyes and put her head on his paw. He licked her head in reassurance and she could hear his steady breathing in her ear. She just hoped The Provider would help her Daddy.

~ * ~

Mute sat staring at the computer screen trying to figure out what he wanted to learn to do next. He saw a white blur and turned to see Valmiki run in. The larger feline bumped Dermot with his large head to get the wolf's attention. Surprised the canine lost his balance and rolled before fumbling back to his feet and showing his teeth.

He wasn't sure what transpired next but Dermot suddenly loped out. Jyotis came in and as he'd seen them do before when one of them was soaked, she added her tongue to her brother's until he was dry. They curled up together afterward in a far corner.

Sasha jumped up and typed. DERMOT JUST TOLD TOMURA HE NEEDED TO GO TO THE MOUNTAINS TO FIND A GHOST HEALER. WORD WARRIOR IS BRINGING BACK A BADLY INJURED WOLF CUB.

HOW SOON? He wanted to know.

WHEN THE STORM STOPS. THAT COULD BE BY SUNSET OR MANY SUNRISES. She stopped briefly and added. MY FATHER WON'T RISK LOSING ANY OF HIS KITTENS AND WON'T LEAVE BEFORE IT'S SAFE .

YOU TOLD ME YOU WERE A FOUNDLING. WHY DO YOU CALL WORD WARRIOR FATHER?

BECAUSE WORD WARRIOR HAS RAISED ME LIKE ONE OF HIS OWN KITTENS.

WHEN YOU COME INTO HEAT, he couldn't believe he was asking this. WON'T HE WANT YOU FOR HIMSELF?

HE TOLD ME I COULD CHOOSE. She held her head up proudly. I HAVE DECIDED AND WILL NOT BE CHALLENGED FOR.

She would not be challenged for? Sasha seemed to be sure about that. Before he could ask who she'd chosen she leapt down and ran out of the room.

~ * ~

When the storm finally stopped many sunrises later, I knew we needed to leave before the next storm, now hovering over the mountains, arrived. If I pushed us we could get back to the school hopefully by sunset. I roused everyone and after a meal of rat we departed.

Unfortunately, the injured wolf moved far too slowly and I feared we would not reach our den before the next approaching storm over took us. I also feared Iden and many of my young might not survive if we were caught on the plains too far from shelter.

We traveled during the light and long into the dark with snow falling on us before reaching the safety of the school. Padding down the hall while my kittens scattered before me, Iden yipped in pain and staggered against the wall.

"What was that noise?" Callie groused as she came out into the hall.

"An injured wolf cub," I responded.

Our Elder flattened her ears and hissed. "Why'd you bring it here?"

My wives stood at the doors of their rooms, my daughters with them, their eyes wide and frightened. My sons ran to join their mothers.

"I would never leave a kitten or a cub to die," I said firmly.

"He didn't leave me to die," Sasha reminded us all.

Pride filled me. She remembered my act of kindness.

"We'd be dead too," Blythe reminded them all, her sister Ellen beside her.

"Should have left it to die," Callie muttered disgustedly.

"Daddy would never do that," Neutron defended me.

Iden panted heavily. We needed to get him to a warm place.

"Come," Tomura ordered. She accompanied Rowena and the cub to the den the wolves had been using.

"Poppin!" I called. "Go get Lavena!"

My kitten scampered away.

"Callie's wrong," Sasha snarled.

I agreed. However, Elders deserved respect. I gently cuffed her with my paw. "Perhaps. Right now I'm hungry. Go hunt me a rat.'

She blinked and replied, "Go hunt it yourself."

⁓ * ⁓

"Did you know Sasha claims she's chosen her mate!" Algier fumed.

Slowly I opened my eyes from my well deserved rest identifying by her scent that Tomura rested beside me. Angrily I stared at the other male. "What do you care? You brought home a mate for yourself."

"And it isn't you!" he taunted.

I knew my first female had always intended for Sasha to become one of my wives.

"You did promise," my wife's soft voice reminded me. "When she came as a kitten you promised she could choose her own mate."

"Stay out of this female!" Algier spat.

"You will *not* speak to Tomura that way!" I hissed back getting to my feet hoping I did not have to fight Algier defending Sasha's choice.

"We always fight for our females!" Algier's blue eyes flamed like very hot fire.

"Sasha has stated her wishes," Tomura calmly informed the other male. "As part of this community, you will honor that."

He snarled.

I asked, "Who did she choose?" I would have to check to see if any other males left urine scents close by.

"When she comes into her first heat," Tomura assured me. "She'll tell you."

"She'll tell me now." I headed for the door to seek out Sasha and hear her choice. I hadn't forgotten her refusal to hunt for me. Such behavior was not tolerable from a female.

"You'll respect her right as a female," Tomura scolded. "Just as I had the right to allow you to challenge." Her thin tail whipped side to side. "I didn't have to."

I knew the truth of her words. She could have mated with the Pureblood who had rightfully won her. Tomura could easily have turned me away. It had been only because of her desire to have her kittens read that she had willingly lowered her status.

"And you," she confronted Algier. "Will stop following her around like she was already yours. You have a wife and kittens coming soon. You need to take care of Sheba first before you add more."

"You aren't my first female," he retorted.

"No. I'm not." She rose to her paws. "But I rule this den. Go against me and I'll chase you off!"

"You wouldn't dare!"

My Siamese wife swiped her claws across his muzzle. He yowled and jumped back, blood dripping from his sensitive nose and splattering on the floor.

"That was a warning!" she hissed.

His tail proudly high, he stalked off. I knew he wouldn't dare challenge Tomura.

"If you force him to leave," I licked my paw. "What about Sheba?"

"His wife is more than welcome to stay. She'll need help with her kittens." My first wife sneezed. "Why he ever challenged for a mate…"

~ * ~

I entered the wolf den. Iden was asleep on what looked like deer hide. Rowena lay beside him. Lavena sat not far away chewing on a large piece of bark.

"Cub needs warmth," the lead female said.

Rowena raised her head. "Maybe Jojo?"

I'd seen Jojo and Nan in the library. "I'll get him." I returned with the pair and Rowena ordered the cub to lay on the other side of Iden. He obeyed. Nan crawled up on her littermate's back. I heard her whisper something about the The Provider to Jojo and wondered what they were talking about.

Rowena squirmed. "I need to relieve myself."

Lavena growled warningly.

"Perhaps one of the Spotted Ghosts could help?" I suggested.

"Yes." Rowena agreed. She rose and trotted warily to the door. Lavena growled again. I knew the dominant female didn't like being disobeyed.

"I'll ask Jyotis if she'll come." Rowena darted out.

"Until the Ghost comes." Lavena padded over and put some of the chewed bark into the cub's mouth. Then she laid down reluctantly beside the cub.

I wisely left the wolves alone.

Chapter 17

Mute stretched his body from the tip of his white tail to his cold wet nose. Sasha, who had napped beside him, simply raised her head, blinked and went back to sleep. Rising slowly trying not to disturb her any more, Mute returned to the computer. He'd managed to find some interesting files and couldn't wait to read them. Tapping in the sequence he'd learned, he watched eagerly as the words scrolled across the screen.

I finally got Veda to sleep. My daughter slept in my arms on the cot. My husband kept my back warm. She made whimpering sounds all night and tears constantly rolled down her face. I understood how she felt. We'd lost everything. Our home. Our friends. Our family.

"We'll survive," my husband had tried to reassure me when we'd come here. "Food is stockpiled. Water too, not to mention the new filtration plant. This place is rigged with a gray water system."

Small comfort when I knew that all the trees, flowers, and animals would die.

"Chasya, living here is not going to be that bad." My husband had put his arms around me. "We have teachers for the children. Even managed to get the greenhouse, or rather hydroponics up and running. Several of the others volunteered to go gather plants and seedlings. We're going to be just fine."

"Are we?" I'd retorted. "The children will never be able to play outside again!" I knew I was crying, which he hates, and I didn't care. "They'll never get to watch a sunset or climb trees." My mind had become numb from all our daughter would never be able to do.

"But we're alive." Kurt had used his convincing tone. I knew it so well. "Be glad you're not watching the casts. People are looting the stores. Shooting each other over what food they can find. Fires are burning out of control. Accidents." He'd kissed my cheek. "It's horrible, Chas."

I tried to push it all aside as Veda shifted beside me, murmuring. I smoothed her black soft hair and hugged her to me. "What are we going to do?" I whispered into the dark room with no windows and hopefully to the One I believed in as well.

The next day I said to Kurt. "Maybe I should have seen them. The casts. Maybe this would be more real to me then."

I somehow sensed what he didn't say. The lucky ones were already dead. For those still trying to survive, death would be slow. They'd starve as crops failed or else they'd freeze for lack of fuel to burn.

"But we'll survive," Kurt told me again. "The human race is resilient. Those who left in the ships, one day, their descendents will come back." He tried to take my hand. I backed away. He bit his lip and continued. "It's not like other governments weren't ready for this. They have shelters, too."

Thoughts about our annoying President resurfaced. I hadn't voted for him. No doubt he, along with the first family, were safely ensconced in some top-secret installation. It made me angry.

"There's a chance some will survive," Kurt informed me as he grabbed a cup of coffee. "This isn't the end, Chas, rather a chance for a new beginning. An opportunity for us to teach our children not to make the same mistakes we did."

How many times had I read that in history books? Besides, I was thinking of a more ancient story, one about a vengeful God, an ark and a great flood.

"We're alive," he smiled at me. "We're in one of the most prepared places you could find! It's going to be great! Just you wait and see!"

A part of me wanted to believe him. Another part - just couldn't.

~ * ~

Kurt finally allowed me to watch some of the holocasts they'd recorded to use as history tools for later generations. The holo seemed unreal almost. Like those idiotic reality shows that were so popular long ago.

I watched as reporters risked their lives filming looters. Objects flew through the air and busted windows. Guns were fired. People carried whatever they could out of the stores and fights broke out between them as they tried to steal from one another.

In the background a mall burned and the fire truck was overturned when it tried to put out the fire. Police were brutally beaten and children, I shuddered at the images, children were trampled by adults, some even run over or worse yet, left crying in the streets.

"That's all we got," Kurt said quietly, sympathy in his voice and on his face. "At least future generations will know what happened."

~ * ~

We still have the cams just outside the base. The temps are falling drastically and it's been snowing for weeks. During all that time I've watched skinny deer trying to strip the dead trees of bark for food. An elk dropped dead outside and a team went outside to skin it for the fresh meat. I've even seen a mountain lion. It was being tracked by some wolves.

Wolves. How long has it been since they thrived here? I remember my grandmother saying in her day there were reports about the wolves coming close to the state border. She was one of the few who hoped they'd be restored to their rightful place during her lifetime. The ranchers and politicians opposed the migration down from Yellowstone. They didn't win, of course. Public opinion did.

My grandmother was a naturalist. She kept notebooks full of her observations. That was one of the few things I managed to bring with me. I missed her terribly. Yet, I'm also glad she didn't live to see me this way. Depressed. Moody. Not wanting to live another day like this.

I'm sitting in our quarters as I write this. Thankfully, Veda is in school. She's one of the few children here. Most couples are now being encouraged to stop using birth control and have more babies. Mustn't allow the human race to die out! Kurt and I are talking about another child. I'm not sure I want to bring another life into this underground world.

Is it fair or even right to condemn our children and theirs, and theirs after, to this place? To this life?

My thoughts are so morbid today. There are so many things we're trying to keep from Veda. Two levels up, a couple committed suicide and poisoned their infant son and toddler daughter. We still don't have an accurate count of the number of people who have just walked outside and froze to death.

Then there are the repeated calls for help over the old radio bands that go silent one by one by one.

Oh, God, what did we do as a race to have earned such an awful punishment? Were we so bad? Will you even allow my daughter to grow up?

~ * ~

Reading my earlier entries I can't believe I was so…negative. We're surviving just fine like Kurt said we would. We've even had more children, another girl and a fine strong son. We named our daughter Serophia. Our boy is Adon, a play on the original Adam.

Veda is growing up fast. Hard to believe she's about to turn thirteen. Kurt is pressuring her to decide on a profession to apprentice. We've been training the teenagers as soon as they choose, before the oldest of us, with all our knowledge, pass on. It's the only way to keep the sciences, history and culture, alive. Not to mention the mechanics we're dependent on.

~ * ~

Mute yawned. He wasn't bored, just tired of reading. He kept finding information but not the actual cause. His search was becoming more and more frustrating. Sasha nipped his ear and she batted at him. She wanted to play.

He jumped down and Sasha joined him on the cold floor. She stretched and pounced on him. They rolled across onto the carpet, kicking at each other with their back feet. When they finally finished playing, they trotted to the cafeteria to catch a rat.

They stalked and chased a large one, teasing it until it couldn't run anymore. He broke its neck and they feasted. After they ate, they cleaned their faces and paws of sticky sweet blood.

Sasha rubbed against him and together they ventured back to the library. She leaped up on the chair and he joined her. Curling together for warmth they drifted off for a well deserved nap. Just before Mute feel asleep, he saw Algier glaring at them from the door.

~ * ~

The moon sat full in the sky, sometimes visible through the thick clouds. Snow no longer fell, but the latest storm had left a thick new layer and high drifts. I stood at the door gazing down the hill, hoping Dermot would return soon with the healer. Lavena was keeping the cub alive, but I feared he might not live for many more sunrises. A rank smell had invaded the wolves' den and I knew the scent—death.

Lavena appeared out of the shadowed hallway. She moved a few body lengths away, squatted, and returned to sit by my side. "Iden has the smell of death," she said. "He has spoken some of his life with the two legs, humans, but I do not think he knows what he says."

"What has he said?" I was curious. All I knew of the two-legged humans was what I had read of them in books or what my mother's elder had shared.

"He says they took other wolves and cats and some of our food animals." She used her teeth to scratch a spot on her shoulder. "Memories we have of humans are not good ones. They hunted us."

"They brought you back, too." Sapphire joined us. Her white fur sparkled under the moon's light.

"They still did not want us," Lavena growled. "We were a threat to their food animals."

"Not all," my daughter informed her. "There were those who understood you were important to the balance."

"That was in the past, Lavena," I told the dominant female.

"Humans do not change." The wolf was firm.

"Maybe," Sapphire ventured, "with not having to compete for the same food animals, they have perhaps, forgotten."

I wondered, only vaguely, where she'd learned that. Had she learned it in class or from reading on her own?

"The only time we were accepted in our memory was when they needed hunting partners. And that was very long ago."

"They kept your descendants as pets." Sapphire cocked her head to one side, much like I have done.

Lavena growled. "You speak of the dogs."

Surprised, I blinked. "The dog gangs were once wolves?"

"Once," she agreed. "The humans decided we could not live with them as we truly were. They changed us to *their* desires until the dogs were no longer wolves."

If that was the true history of the wolves, I began to ponder what they had done to us. I remembered stories by my mother's elder about being worshipped in a place called Egypt. Yet, nothing else was known. Had the two-legs, humans, tried to do the same with us? My body shivered at the fearful thought.

"Dermot needs to hurry." Lavena voiced my earlier thought. "Wepwawet hovers near Iden."

I tried to reassure her. "Dermot will return as quickly as he can." I found myself silently asking The Provider to be merciful and either spare the cub or take it quickly in death.

She didn't answer. Rather, the howls of her pack began and she lifted her muzzle to the sky and joined them. Their chorus belonged together and she left us to join them.

More howling echoed down the hallway. I heard Rowena and Jojo's voices. How lonely the two sounded, even if they were together. It was broken by a painful yowl and I ran with my daughter down to their den.

"In the name of Bast!" Tomura raced to join us.

"In pain…" Iden whined.

Rowena chewed more bark and fed it to Iden. He quieted soon after and closed his eyes. His tongue hung out and he panted, as if each breath were difficult. Jojo crept to the young wolf's side and whined.

I understood the cub's fear and prayed again to The Provider for Dermot's quick return.

~ * ~

Mute smelled the difference, similar to rat blood, yet different. It drew him, made his heart beat faster and filled him with a desire he didn't fully understand.

Sasha rubbed against him and stepped away almost as if she were teasing him. He followed as she drew him away from the library and into one of the rooms. She crouched down, her rear high.

He sensed the invitation, but before he could accept, Algier attacked him. The two rolled across the dirty floor, getting dust into their fur, and out into the hallway. Sasha was suddenly between them, her claws raking across the other male's muzzle.

Word Warrior dashed in and Mute knew a moment of fear. Would the leader of the den also challenge him? The large male grabbed Algier by the neck and dragged him back from Mute. Algier spat at Word Warrior and tried once again to attack Mute. Word Warrior bit the other male on the leg.

Several females raced in putting themselves in a protective circle around Sasha and Mute. The younger male watched as the two older males viciously fought. They seemed almost evenly matched. Word Warrior scored a raking tear across gray-striped fur and Algier slunk away in defeat.

The large male stood panting. He did not approach Mute or Sasha. He only gave the younger white male an approving look as if giving his permission and left, the proud lead female at his side, the others following behind.

Sasha licked Mute's wounds and the two returned to their mating.

~ * ~

Mute opened his blue eyes and met Nan's intense stare. With Sasha's help he was slowly learning who each cat and kitten was. His mate stirred beside him and she lifted herself up, stretching, and stopping to lick a spot on her back. She and Nan seemed to have some sort of exchange and they ran out of the room.

He slowly rose and stretched himself. An intense cold invaded his nose and he shivered. Another storm must have blown in. Padding down the hall he found a window and jumped up. All he could see was a blinding white obscuring everything else.

Returning to the floor, he went to the cafeteria, hunted a rat, and went to his favorite place in the school, the library. Once again sitting in front of the computer he typed in a command. He'd read somewhere about old satellites orbiting the planet and sending back information. That brought another question to his mind, how long had this winter gone on and did the humans have any idea on when it might end?

He had some understanding of the old dating system they'd used. The more he thought about it the more he wondered if the winter would end in his lifetime, or his kittens, or theirs after, or?

His kittens. Now that realization was taking some time to get used to.

The screen went gray and he scratched his ear. There must be a problem reaching the satellites. Maybe the storm was somehow interfering. He'd read that happened.

Sasha joined him and typed.

SHEBA HAD HER KITTENS. TWO MALES AND A FEMALE. SHE NAMED THEM POLE, ROOG, AND MIST.

STRANGE NAMES, he typed back.

SHE WANTED DIFFERENT NAMES. COME WITH ME AND SEE THEM.

He joined his mate and two quietly entered the gym. Sheba merely blinked at him and he gazed into her nest at the three small bodies. Their eyes were closed and they sucked at her tits.

Soon, he too, would have young to help care for. He didn't quite know how he felt about becoming a father. It was still too new to him. He'd have to spend some time with Word Warrior. The older male took excellent care of his females and kittens.

Sasha rubbed her head against his side. He followed her out. She went to find a rat and he returned to the library. He stared at the screen for a long time, wondering what else he could do with the computer. Shifting his attention to the instruction book he'd found he settled down to read.

Chapter 18

Dermot finally returned after many sunsets with a full-grown Spotted Ghost. He introduced the healer as Indrani. From what he told me, she'd met him at the edge of the city and had known he needed her.

"The Ghosts are concerned about the metal monsters invading the peaks and valleys," he growled deep in his throat. "Several cubs have been taken and many wolves have died."

"I told you how it would be," Lavena reminded me. "They hate us."

We stood in the hall outside the wolves' den. I looked around the canines to watch the Ghost. She cleaned the burns with her tongue, chewing on the bark and some other plants and then applying them to the stinking skin.

"Wepwawet hovers and waits." Lavena's crouched low. Her body reflected her fear.

"True, death hovers near," Indrani agreed. "But Sekhmet is a powerful warrior and healer. She battles for the young one."

"Will he live?" I wanted to know, puzzled at the mention of a new goddess.

"I do not know." She laid down beside the young wolf. "I will do what I can."

We moved further down the hall and away from hovering death.

"They are in the mountains. They have been here." Lavena barked harshly to make her point. "They will return again. We must decide what we will do."

"We'll meet later," I answered her.

"I'll inform the packs." She trotted away.

Dermot glanced after her. "The humans. They do not understand we are intelligent. I do not think they want to know."

Deep down, a very primitive part of me agreed.

~ * ~

The dominants plus Dermot and Indrani joined me later as the sun rose. We held our meeting in the library. Tomura draped herself in the chair to listen and I noticed Mute reading a book on the counter. I'd have to ask Sasha later what new things he was teaching himself.

Phelan growled. "Lavena has told us of the humans and where they have been. They took a pup."

"And they're killing us," Sloan added.

Yseult spoke up. "One of their flying metal monsters crashed near here. When the humans do not return, they will come to see why."

"True," Indrani agreed.

"Then we should kill them." Phelan bared his teeth.

Indrani's yellow eyes seemed to look at us all. "Ancient memories suggest killing humans is dangerous. Kill one, and they will send more. Do you wish for us all to die?"

I felt a shiver that had nothing to do with the cold. In some of the books I'd read, they talked of the species they'd wiped out.

Herne lifted his large white paw and butted Phelan with it. He shook his gray head. "Not a wise plan."

"Agreed," Lavena quickly backed her mate, despite what I knew of her own thoughts on this matter. I'd learned from Rowena that was one way they kept unity and order in the pack.

"I won't lose any of my pack to humans!" Yseult objected.

Her mate Sloan was briefly silent before he suggested, "Perhaps it would be best if we left. Spread ourselves out in the valley, make it harder for the humans to find us."

"Didn't stop them from taking a cub before," Cara softly put in. "We lived in our own territories then."

"Cara has a point," Dermot agreed, though I knew he would have little say.

A deep chilling quiet filled the room. I knew the wolves were debating the point and I hoped, remembering why we had all come together to begin with, our common welfare would influence their decision.

Tomura's voice drifted down. "The burned out machine is far from here. I do not think they will come to the school looking for answers."

"Humans are curious creatures, just like us." Indrani wrapped her long spotted tail over her paws. "They will come to see to their dead."

"We should stay far from the wreck," Dermot advised.

"We must know what they do!" Yseult emphasized.

I said, "Perhaps one of us could go there and watch when they come."

"A good idea." Cara surprisingly backed my idea.

The others finally reluctantly agreed, but I knew they did not like it and wondered what would come of this decision.

~ * ~

Lavena threw up some deer meat for Iden to eat. The cub nibbled a couple of bites and fell back to sleep. I understood their ways, but the smell of undigested meat was disgusting.

"He is feeling better," Indrani commented. She sniffed at his burns. "Weak still."

"Iden will live?" I dared to start thinking he would.

"Death no longer hovers. Sekhmet has won the battle for now. There is always the possibility it could return. The goddess will stay vigilant." Her eyes turned to me and drifted to the meat. She grabbed some of the contents of Lavena's stomach. "Good meat."

"Brought for cub, not you," Lavena growled.

"The cub will have some left," the Ghost promised.

"Better." Lavena warned as she left the room.

I left as well to join Starlite. My wife sat on one of the window ledges, watching yet another storm cover the ground. Her kittens were studying with Algier.

"Our future is uncertain." She blinked her blue eyes, her gaze shifted to include me.

"Your 'sight' tells you this?" I easily jumped up and sat, my tail out behind me.

"I see many things." Starlite looked back outside. "The world again filled with humans, the dogs beside them. Small dogs though. Not the huge ones in the gangs." Her tone was sad. "I don't see us."

"You don't see us at all?"

"Yes…and no. I see other visions, but they are unclear." She cleaned a spot on her back. "I am not certain, but I think I see my mother. How is that possible since I do not remember her?"

Much about her mother, other than the little Callie knew, was unknown. Sometimes, our Elder would share the strange stories Starlite's mother had told.

"Perhaps you see the world where our spirits go to rejoin," I hesitated since my beliefs were now different than my wives.

"No. I have briefly glimpsed that world. These are different." She laid down and put her head on her paws. I heard the bell she wore chime softly.

"What else have you seen?" I hoped she could tell me more about the immediate future. That's the information I really needed.

"Many things. I don't always understand them." She lifted her head. "It's important. For all felines."

"Starlite," I inquired gently. "What will happen when the humans find the burned machine?"

"Mute is part of the answer." She rose again to her feet.

I knew I would not get anymore from her. I leaped down and glanced back. Starlite stood, her body swaying making sounds I'd never heard before, the bell matching her odd song. Vibrations wiggled through my skin into my bones. I wanted to join her and flee at the same time. For a brief heartbeat, I thought I stood somewhere else. It vanished and when I looked at my wife again, she slept.

~ * ~

Sasha lifted her head from where she rested on the chair as I entered the room. She flipped her tail in irritation.

"Where's Mute?"

"The computer. Where else?"

I leaped up and found the younger male placing his paws on various letters. "How do I talk to him?" I demanded of Sasha.

Slowly she got up, stretched and joined us. "I'll show you." She typed, WORD WARRIOR WANTS TO TALK WITH YOU.

ABOUT WHAT?

Quickly I told Sasha what Starlite had told me. She informed Mute.

WHY TELL ME? Mute looked at me.

Why indeed? Maybe I hoped he might have some idea about how he could help us avoid the humans who I was certain would come.

~ * ~

Mute paused reading his book. He watched as Sasha jumped off her chair to pounce on Nan. Nan swatted back and a game of chase started with Jojo playfully joining in. He watched from above amused as the wolf tried to catch Nan and she kept wiggling under a shelf and getting away.

His mate left the game and sauntered out of the library. He figured she went to build her nest. Sasha had been adding pieces of wool since their mating.

Mute considered trying some of the new operations he'd learned. He found he really wasn't interested and decided to go hunting.

Nan and Jojo dashed out the door before him. He let them pass and went to the cafeteria. Finding a lone rat, he stalked it, killed it, and took his meal back to the room he now shared with Sasha. His mate napped on her expanding nest and he ate his rat, leaving her a choice part for when she woke.

Restless, he left again, going back to the library. Taking his spot in front of the computer, he debated what to do next. He sensed sometimes Sasha didn't approve of all the time he spent with the machine even though it allowed them to communicate with each other.

Thinking of his mate, he knew how happy she'd made him by choosing him. He no longer felt like he was abandoned and not wanted. He had not forgotten the pain left by the deaths of his two mothers. And yet too, he carried the memories of their tongues that had cleaned him, milk that had fed him, and their reassuring vibrations.

Mute had no doubt his foster mother had died to protect him and the cubs as well. He missed her and hoped whatever deity she believed in, had rewarded her. He hoped the same for his mother.

He jumped down and wandered over to the chair thinking now would be a good time for a nap. However, with the sense of loss he felt, he reconsidered and went to join his mate instead.

~ * ~

"I think Iden will live," Indrani informed me as she came into the room I was resting in.

Glancing at her from my place on the windowsill, I slowly stretched. It had been many sunrises since she'd come to take care of Iden. Iden had eaten more of the contents of Lavena's stomach she kept providing him. At least he was getting stronger finally.

Hurried clicks sounded and I recognized the sound of a wolf's stride. Jojo bounced in like Nan often did and stopped short. His long pink tongue licked his thin black lips. "The packs, they're leaving."

The packs were leaving? Had I heard him correctly?

I rushed out, running down the dark hallway and into the cold. Entering the side building, I found the dominant pairs. Yseult growled. Sloan stepped in front of her, his snarl equally menacing.

"Jojo told me you were leaving!" I couldn't believe it. But, as I thought back, I hadn't seen any of the wolf cubs in classes for several sunrises.

"We are," Phelan confirmed.

"That hasn't fully been decided," Cara interjected.

"Yes. It has." Yseult nipped at the other female. "I will not stay here and be killed!"

"Nor will I!" Sloan confirmed.

"Go if you wish." Herne stepped beside me. "But Lavena and I will stay."

"Then you'll die!" Sloan loped out, his mate beside him. The rest of the pack followed them.

Phelan stood by the door. "Come, Cara. We too shall leave."

"You can go. I chose to stay."

He hesitated. "If you don't go with me, I will choose another mate."

Lavena's low growl filled the room in defense of her daughter. "You would not dare!"

"He has the right," she reminded her mother. "You can go, Phelan, but the pups stay."

Her mate moved to as if to attack her, only to find Lavena and Herne between them. "Very well," Phelan consented. He called to the rest of the pack and they ran out the door, down the hill and were gone. The pups tried to follow, but Cara stopped them.

She woofed with disdain. "Phelan allowed his fear to decide. He is not worthy to be my mate." Her clear eyes met mine. "As is our way, I am not allowed to rejoin my mother's pack. I ask to be allowed to be part of yours. My pups as well."

I had never thought of my mates, young, the wolves, and the Spotted Ghosts, as a pack. But I could understand, from her perspective, how she might think so.

"Of course," I heard myself tell her.

"We are staying," Herne reassured me.

"My pups will be back in class at next sunrise," Lavena told me. "I kept them away while the packs decided." Her head dipped. "Even some of my pack left."

"Their fear was too strong," Herne barked. "It is better they are gone. Only the bravest remained. We will have a stronger pack."

And hopefully, so would our community.

~ * ~

What happened with the packs spread quickly. Many of the females in the nearby houses came to talk with us. They were greatly concerned.

"We are worried," asked a tiny black female.

"Lavena and Herne stayed," I answered.

"I thought they would help protect us!" a long haired white hissed.

"We can hide." Mitzy glanced at me with fear in her eyes. "We've done it before."

"If the humans return…we're all in danger!" The cry came from a female heavy with kittens.

My heart beat faster and I tasted the same fear as the wolves. I feared losing all we had built.

"Running is for the weak." Cara loped in. Several of the females scattered out of her way. "True strength lies in staying together."

"Your pack left you." The small black again.

"True," she quietly agreed. "They left in fear, and once they run, they will never stand strong as a pack again."

"We aren't like the packs." The female who spoke looked as if she might be a Mau.

"No." My tail flicked. "We aren't."

Starlite came and sat beside me. The others fell silent. The females all knew she had the 'sight' and now they chose to listen. I knew my mate's words carried great influence.

"Change always comes creeping upon us as we stalk a rat. The two legs might be a danger to us. Or they might not." She stood, her fur glistening like silver, sparkling in the fading light. "We have stories of the past told to us by our Elders." She turned her gaze to Callie. "Vague are our memories on how or whether we lived together or apart from them."

Hisses answered her statement and a couple of yowls.

"Meeting with them now, with such a vague history, brings questions we will not be able to answer. Yet Bast, in all her wisdom, has not given us a clear choice."

I felt an odd tug of unease, but pushed it aside to listen to my wife's words.

"So you do not know what our fate will be?" Tomura met Starlite's gaze.

"Bast has closed the door and I cannot see clearly." Starlite regally sat with her tail tucked around her paws. "We can but wait and trust the goddess. She has chosen for us. I believe," she rose and turned in a circle, the bell she wore chiming, "She will continue to protect us. She did not give us a gift to have it stolen."

Was it really the goddesses who gave us the gift? Or The Provider?

Chapter 19

Mute missed Sasha. She'd explained to him there was a meeting of the felines because many of the wolves had chosen to leave. She promised to tell him later what had been said.

Cleaning a bit of blood off his muzzle from his recent rat kill, he headed back to the library. He was thankful Word Warrior had taken in Sasha, himself, and many others. The male had learned valuable lessons from human examples. Normally, from what he'd learned from his mate, males killed kittens not their own and chased away any potential rival males.

He glanced in the room where the meeting was taking place. He didn't know what was going on, but Word Warrior seemed to be making a point. The females listened intently and soon dispersed. Sasha met him and took him to the computer and told him what happened. Word Warrior, with Starlight's help, had managed to keep the community that had been built together, despite the wolves leaving.

~ * ~

Weak sunlight streamed down on the concrete and I heard the faint drip as snow melted off the roof onto the ground. My nose didn't detect storm scent. We finally had a break in the series of storms which had dumped even more snow on us.

The outcome of the meeting, though the community was still together, still held a sense of uncertainty. It troubled me.

"Is this a good hunting day, Daddy?" Nan asked me.

My daughter, now almost grown, bronze and beautiful like her mother, stood in the door. Jojo was beside her and I thought it sad he was a canine. The two inseparable friends would suit each other for mating.

"Yes." My heart began to pick up. The prospect of running and hunting excited me. Maybe we could find prey to give us a break in eating rat.

"Goody!" She bounded out, Jojo right behind her. The two floundered down the hill and chased each other into a small gully.

I followed more slowly, testing the surface. Not that I really needed to worry, the large paws I'd inherited from my father, worked well on the snow.

Traversing the gully we reached the open field. Nan and Jojo raced across it, forgetting to be silent. Several rabbits dashed back into their holes. The young wolf dug at one and a rabbit hopped out another entrance.

Seeing its movement, I hid behind a tree trunk, and pounced when it reached me. I broke its neck and paused to see if they'd had any luck. Jojo had one hanging from his large mouth. Nan hadn't caught anything, but didn't seem to care. We took our kills back to school and I shared mine with my wives and Callie.

We all took advantage of the rare sunlight after our meal. My wives and I lounged on the cold concrete and my young played in the snow, the wolf cubs joining them. Games of chase, hide and pounce commenced.

Lavena and Herne had taken the pack to hunt, leaving the growing cubs in Cara's care. She, along with Dermot and Rowena, joined us, laying down and resting, yet keeping alert in the event one of the cubs needed them.

The two Spotted Ghosts also joined in the games. They were very careful when playing with my kittens. Their large paws could easily snap fragile feline necks or backs.

"To be young again," Indrani lamented as the female stepped outside, watching the youngsters with envious yellow eyes.

"There is much to be said for being dignified," Tomura replied.

"Speak for yourself," Starlite retorted, getting up and joining the fun.

Lara cleaned a spot on her shoulder, taking great care to groom her fur with her teeth, before smoothing her black fur back into place. She lazily blinked her copper eyes. "I enjoy the time away from my kittens."

"I do as well." Mitzy's tail tip flipped lazily.

Hearing a sound behind us, I noticed one of the wolf cubs grab some carpet and the kittens began to sled down the hill. It was their favorite game and I hoped they'd get to play it for as long as they wanted.

Other females joined us, their kittens frolicking with mine. I noticed the number and suddenly realized that soon, we would have to expand beyond the walls of the school. Still the shadow of the humans, the two legs, returning, could mean we would have to move the entire community. That would take many sunrises and would require the help of all. We would need to move the books. Not to mention finding a new place for them all to live, a safe place from the dog gangs, the constant storms, and to be able to raise our kittens as we wished.

Did I dare trust what 'little' Starlite saw of our future? The entire fate of the felines, wolves and Spotted Ghosts, rested on her visions and my trust in her. Or should I ask The Provider what to do?

Rowena and Dermot tumbled in the snow, the two dashing after each other like kittens. I washed a spot on my neck, occasionally glancing up to watch them. I heard a faint growl from Cara, but ignored it. The weather was too good not to enjoy it.

~ * ~

The weather continued to favor us. For several sunrises there had been no new storms. All of us had gone outside to enjoy the crisp fresh air after the classes had finished.

"Rowena will soon come into season," Lavena commented.

I paused in my washing to listen. Rowena was coming into heat?

"What?" Cara lifted her gray head. She turned her muzzle in their direction.

"Can't you sense it?" the dominant female inquired.

Cara growled deep in her throat. "He should be chasing me."

"You haven't been in their pack long enough, Cara. At least they accepted you." Lavena sounded puzzled. I knew it was not the way of the packs to accept a full grown wolf, but Rowena, Dermot, Iden and Jojo, had taken her in along with her pups.

"It still should be me." She pushed herself up.

"Rowena is the dominant female of her pack. You should understand this," Lavena instructed her daughter. "Dermot is the strongest male. It is their choice."

"I've held the position. I should pee on Rowena."

"Cara," her mother warned.

The younger female ignored her mother and attacked Rowena. I watched in horror as the two fought, their fierce snarls reaching my ears. Many of my young ran inside, others huddled around me or their mothers. The wolf cubs simply sat, awaiting the outcome. I glanced over at the Spotted Ghosts. They were cleaning their paws and ignoring the fight.

It wasn't a very long fight from what I observed. Rowena pinned Cara by her sleek neck, locking it in her powerful jaws. I knew from experience she could kill a large prey animal with them.

"Yield, Cara," Dermot ordered. He'd wisely stayed out of the fight. "You will abide by the rules of the pack."

"Usurper," she replied, kicking with her back paws.

"You're the newest in our pack and have yet to earn your proper place." I could tell Dermot was not going to be patient with the female. "If you don't like it, go find yourself a new male."

Cara wiggled trying to get up. Rowena held on tight and growled.

"Yield," the young female finally conceded.

Relieved the conflict was over; I continued to listen, though I pretended not to by pulling at my loose claws.

Rowena released the other female. Dermot came over to her, sniffing to make certain his chosen mate was uninjured. Together the pair trotted down the hill.

The defeated female slunk back to her mother's side, licking at the few wounds she'd received.

"Dermot's right," Lavena said. "If you wish to rule a pack again, you must seek a new mate."

Cara's blue eyes glared, watching the pair jealously. "Be quiet, Mother."

A part of me sensed that perhaps, this conflict was not entirely at an end. Tomura rubbed her sleek body against me. "They too have their challenges."

"They do," I agreed.

"What troubles you, my husband?"

"I do not think this matter is settled."

"I can understand how Cara feels," my wife sympathized. "I would not want to lose my place as your first female."

"You're in no danger of that," I reassured her. "For Cara, it isn't the same."

"Perhaps not. But she made her choice when she left her pack."

I had to agree Tomura had a point though I do not think Cara fully understood the consequences of her decision.

"She'll find a new place," Jojo broke into our conversation. Nan stood beside him.

I jumped back. I hadn't heard him approach. He was normally more noisy and easy to hear.

"Cara doesn't like it much." His brown eyes glowed. "Indrani says in a few more sunrises she thinks Iden will be well enough, she'll no longer need to be near constantly."

I was relieved the young wolf would recover. When I had first seen him, I did not truly think he would live.

Jojo lifted his muzzle and watched Rowena and Dermot. "They will lead our pack well."

"Daddy," Nan said. "I think Jojo and I should go and watch to see if the two-legs come to the dead metal thing."

"No, Nan." I feared for her even though I knew Jojo would protect her.

"Someone must go," she insisted.

"I will think on it and when I have made my decision, I will tell you."

My daughter seemed content with my answer. The pair padded off together to join the others in play.

~ * ~

Mute sat staring at the computer. There were a few more programs he wanted to try, including something called 'email'. He wasn't sure it would do them any good, yet he wanted to understand all he could about the computer's different operations.

Agilely he jumped down and went in search of Sasha. She'd been spending more time than normal preparing and rearranging the nest. Mute entered the sun lit room they shared. His mate gazed calmly at him, her head resting on her gray paws.

Greeting her nose to nose, he didn't join her in the nest for a nap. Instead, he leaped up on the windowsill to look out. The sun had warmed a spot making it a much more inviting place to nap. He laid down, his white body relaxing.

No wind blew and the trees didn't sway or, as they tended to do, snap and bust into pieces. And there was no storm today. He couldn't see any of the other cats. They must not be in the area.

His eyes traveled up the snow covered expanse to the deserted playground. He concentrated trying to recall what the various objects were called. Swings, one side broken, a slide, teeter-totters shaped like odd creatures, the paint pealed and cracked, bars, a bit of black. Could be the seat of the teeter tooter or another swing, or perhaps the handle of the buried sandbox.

His explorations hadn't uncovered a map, blue print the humans had called them, for the school and grounds. He had some idea how the building was laid out from late nights of prowling and hunting. There were still some rooms to expand and den in, especially with two of the wolf packs gone. Also, there were plenty of houses they could use. He could see them out of almost every window.

The bit of black moved. Mute lifted his head. Now it skitted around the edge of the brick building, an obvious feline head up and alert.

Instinctively, he pulled back his lips in a silent challenge.

Without thinking he followed the intruder's movements until it reached the ledge of his windowsill. Mute leaped down and raced down the hall and outside. He vaguely noticed the others hop aside as he surprised them by running past. He had to head off the other cat. Pressing low into the snow, he hoped he would blend in and not be seen. His tail whipped in anger as he waited, his body tense and ready for battle.

The black shadow flowed around a corner, sharp gold eyes carefully surveying the area, and slinking forward. Mute stayed quiet knowing his chance for the perfect ambush would come only once. He dared not miss!

Chapter 20

Mute rushing by surprised us all. I immediately knew the den must be in danger or he would have sent Sasha with a message. Like all males, he was acting in self defense.

"Tomura, get my kittens and wives inside!" I didn't stay to see if I was obeyed.

I slipped around the corner of the building noting an impression in the snow. If I hadn't seen a slight move, I would never have known it was Mute. I pressed against the brick knowing it would hide me from whatever danger approached.

Something black crept around a far corner, lifting a feline head, sniffing for betraying scents, bright eyes checking to see if he'd been detected. I had no doubt it was an invading male. My heart beat much faster and the battle heat filled my veins. I may not have had to fight recently to defend my females and kittens, but by The Provider, I had not forgotten how!

Mute slowly raised up, one paw slightly elevated, ready to strike. He dashed low over the snow and leaped on the skulking male. The two rolled and tumbled before separating. They circled each other, each seeking a potential weakness in order to strike. Well, did I know the tactic.

I hissed for I knew the movements of the intruder. Midnight! My old rival snarled, perplexed his challenge yowl went unanswered by Mute.

Midnight quickly tired of circling and dodged low trying to get one of Mute's feet. The young male seemed to anticipate the move and he bit Midnight's paw instead.

The older cat managed to sink his teeth into Mute's shoulder and it looked as if the battle might be over.

I didn't hesitate. I lunged for Midnight's neck before he could get a death grip on Mute. He fell over but got to his feet before I could find my mark. We circled, leaving a body length between us, the fur on our backs high.

"Taking in another male," Midnight spat at me. "He'll take what is yours."

"He earned his place," I retorted, watching both my opponent and the younger male. Mute managed to escape and stood several bodies lengths away watching us. His tail flicked side to side.

"Should have run him off!" If Midnight had truly understood why the younger male was of such great value, he would not have chosen the words he had. I had no doubt he was trying to distract me.

"After I rid myself of you." Midnight crouched low to the ground, getting ready for a killing pounce. "I'll kill him as well."

For whatever reason, he did not use the move I thought he was going to. Instead he rammed me with his head, upsetting my balance. My body fell into the snow and I floundered. Desperately I tried to get to my feet before he could grip my throat. He raked my side as he leaped. I flopped ungracefully before his teeth could find my throat.

"You took not only the best," Midnight accused, trying to back me into a position where I would have no defense. "But you convinced the females they could do better. They no longer honor the proper way of challenge and victory." He came at me wildly, his claws finding my skin to shred and mark.

I heard Midnight screech and saw Mute jump. The smell of blood filled my nose and I knew the younger male wounded our rival. The Bombay whirled slashing a deep cut on Mute's face and he slunk back defeated. The intruder again turned his full attention to me again.

Fortunately, Mute's attack gave me time to get back on my feet.

"You filled their heads full of useless book learning." His eyes blazed with a madness I'd only seen with the frothing sickness. "When I kill you, your kittens will be next!"

"You'll do no such thing!" Tomura's beautiful bronze body suddenly was between us. She voiced a full battle challenge.

"You try and harm *my* kittens and I'll snap your neck myself!" Lara roared. She placed herself beside Tomura.

Mitzy bounded out as did Starlite, each taking a stance behind the other male. He was surrounded by my wives. I saw Sasha run past to Mute.

"That goes for us as well," Mitzy warned, her tail leaving an impression in the snow as she whipped it in anger. "We made the choice to become his mates. He has much more to offer than you. Or any other male."

"We are the future," Starlite added. "Your ways are now past. Ours will rule when the time of snow and cold are past."

I staggered up unsure what I should do. Females had never intervened in a direct challenge before.

"You stupid females!" Midnight screamed.

"Not as stupid as you would like." We all turned to look at Callie. She stood a few body lengths away, her old voice carrying authority. "You should leave."

"Yes, go," Tomura ordered.

Midnight tried to spring at me. Tomura and Lara didn't move. Lara scored a rake across his nose. He hissed in response.

"Go," Tomura repeated, her chocolate eyes reflecting her deep fury.

The Bombay made a pretend move to comply, only to turn his anger on Mute. Sasha jumped the other male and my females joined in. Used to only fighting other males one to one, Midnight couldn't fend off multiple attackers. Bloody and sorely beaten, he fled for his life, running past the ancient playground, with Lara and Mitzy in pursuit.

Tomura warned him as he ran. "You tell other males foolish enough to try and challenge our husband; we'll do the same to them!"

Lara and Mitzy chased him to the distant fence before returning.

My wives surrounded me licking my wounds. I shakily accompanied them into the school where Tomura insisted I rest in her nest and Lara brought me a rat.

"What about Mute?" I asked as my eyes closed.

"Sasha is caring for him." Pride filled Tomura's voice. "I trained her well."

~ * ~

I awoke to Nan's insistent cries. "Daddy! Daddy! You have to come and see!"

Stiff and sore in places unfamiliar to me, I cautiously stretched. Nan waited by the door with Tomura. Slowly I walked to them and we joined the others outside. Dark had fallen. The partial pale moon hung in the sky, yet a veiling mist shrouded its light shaded in tones of red, yellow, green, blue, and purple. They almost seemed to spark.

Algier spoke beside me. "I found a book." He lazily licked his paw and wiped at his muzzle before continuing. "Humans theorized what it might be like if we moved too close to the asteroid belt."

Vaguely I found myself wondering where'd he'd been during Midnight's challenge. Yet, a part of me decided it wasn't important. The Provider had reasons for events coming to pass as they did.

"What he means," Neutron explained. "Is that sometimes the Earth is in an elliptical orbit."

Not that I understood my kitten's explanation any better than Algier's. My body hurt and all I wanted to do was return to sleep.

"It doesn't go around the sun like it's supposed to," Algier snapped. He must have picked up my thought.

Neutron went on. "I think, maybe, we might be passing through the extreme outer edge of the belt." My son didn't sound very sure of that.

I left the mysteries of astronomy and science to Algier's teaching and those of my kittens who grasped it.

"That's what the lights are," Sapphire added. "Small bits of rocks hitting the upper atmosphere."

"They're pretty." Blythe gazed dreamily above.

Nan's soft voice surprised us all by lifting in song, Jojo howling in harmony.

How she sounded so much like her mother when she sang!

"Protected in fur
we watch the sky
colorful comets
streaking over our heads.

Endless black filling the dark
beckoning with fabled jeweled delight,
spoken of in books written
by long dead humans.

Sapphires, rubies, emeralds,
diamonds, amber and gold.

Gold. Our gold.
Receding further
like leaving a hunt
returning with the sunrise
with no prey.

Winter's daunting hand
replaced with sharp cold claws,

warm nest further taken
perhaps not to return
during our memory."

My daughter's song held a sadness touching deep into my soul. No doubt, as I well knew from reading human books, they brought dreams and desires to live in a world full of warm days, trees we could climb and grass we could lie in or hide to stalk prey. Some things from the past we'd never know, nor our kittens, nor theirs. How much longer the seemingly endless winter would last, we had no way of knowing. None of the records we found had spoken of an end.

We watched the lights well into the dark before scattering. Some of my young went off to hunt rabbits, while others returned to various rooms to continue learning or to sleep. I slowly got up, extremely tired, hurting and wanting to return to the warmth of Tomura's nest and my much needed rest. My wife went with me and she curled her body beside me.

When I awoke, Tomura had moved to the windowsill allowing the sun to warm her. I stretched again, noticing my many sore spots.

"You've slept long, husband," my first wife greeted me.

The rest was much needed to speed my healing.

"Lara left you another rat."

Finding the rodent a body length away, I tasted the raw flesh and ate until my hunger left. I licked my paw and cleaned my face.

"How's Mute?" I leaped up to join my mate.

"Recovering. He was not hurt as badly as you."

"Good." I would have to find a way to thank him later for the warning. The younger male had saved many lives with his brave actions.

"Sasha will have her kittens soon."

Sprawling across the chilly top I wondered how Tomura knew.

"Her nest is completed," she answered almost as if she read my mind, like Algier. "A clear sign she will birth soon."

More kittens added to our growing community.

"We females have noticed that the younger ones are now many moonrises older before they come into their first heat." She licked my muzzle affectionately. "Algier seems to think this is a natural evo...lution for us." Tomura hesitated over the unknown word.

A curious change. "He told you that?" I didn't know if I liked the fact he had talked to my wives.

"I've been attending his science classes. He's teaching evolutionary," she said the word much clearer, "change and how it helps us survive. He thinks that is part of what is happening to us."

"Does his teaching say it is a good thing?"

"Yes and no." Her tail lifted and settled again. "It will give our young more time to learn before they have to raise their own kittens."

Something I had not considered nor the advantages to us.

"A very good change for us all," Tomura concluded, blinking lazily.

I noticed she had not gone into the 'no' part of her reply. And then, I began to wonder if the other males had noticed these changes as well? Was that why Midnight had made such a bold attack against me? Were his females still raising kittens and not ready for a new mating soon enough so he could increase his young? Had he thought that by killing my kittens the females would come into heat faster?

Exasperated I stopped the line of thinking. Without being able to directly ask him, I would not ever have a way of knowing. I knew he hated me and my young, and that my wives had more freedom than most females. A freedom others were slowly claiming by bringing their kittens here to have them educated.

Or had Midnight perhaps just wanted the rule of challenge and mate to stay?

A part of me understood we were no longer those same felines. It hadn't been just me who learned to Read, but also Mute who had brought with him the mystery of Writing. Lara who had come with to me knowing Math and Algier the Science. By bonding together we had changed the destiny of all felines.

Chapter 21

Mute understood his mate Sasha was in pain. He wanted to help and honestly didn't know how. He sat next to her nest as her body strained to deliver their kittens. At last, a small head appeared and the kitten dropped out. Sasha quickly severed the umbilical cord with her teeth and broke open the thin membrane around it. She washed the nose and mouth so it could breathe. After she fully cleaned the kitten, she gently nudged it to her tit so it could nurse. She then delivered her second, repeating the process, and also a third.

Affectionately he licked her face, and lay on the opposite side of her to offer his warmth, so he wouldn't crush their kittens as they ate. He was now a father and proudly understood how Word Warrior must have felt.

Sasha's body rumbled. He knew she was both comforting and welcoming her kittens. He wondered what she would name them and knew it might be a long while before she typed their names on the computer so he would know. He also knew she would not leave the nest except to hunt or relieve herself. From Word Warrior's example Mute could help his mate by hunting for Sasha and keeping kittens warm when she was away.

Content and happy for probably the first time in his life, Mute felt his own body rumble.

~ * ~

I stopped in the doorway watching Mute and Sasha with their kittens. The younger male had just brought in a rat and his mate daintily nibbled at it. Noticing movement I was not surprised to see Nan and Jojo peering curiously at the new additions.

Jojo approached and stuck his long nose in the nest. Mute swatted him and the wolf darted away.

"Nan," Sasha patiently asked. "Please, take Jojo away. My kittens are not old enough for him to see yet."

"Okay." Nan spoke to her friend. He panted, yipped, and chased her down the hall.

I went down the hall and stopped at the room the Spotted Ghosts had made their own. The two younger ones were almost full grown and Indrani had been instructing them in the importance of stalking, what was food and what wasn't, where to den, mating, and other things they needed to know to survive.

Tomura had taken over the instruction of teaching the younger kittens how to read. Even more females had arrived, denning in the surrounding houses, and the school was becoming more and more crowded. Perhaps it was time to find a new den for ourselves, leaving the school to be what the humans had built it for—a place of learning.

Even Algier and Sheba had left their gym nest and taken their kittens to a house not far away and not inhabited by any of the females. "Too much noise," the other male had complained. "My head always hurts."

I now understood. Perhaps I should be thinking of finding a suitable house for my wives, and me, and the new kittens who would be born when they came into heat again. A good choice considering my older kittens would soon be thinking about mating. Already I had noticed certain ones pairing. No challenges had been issued, just mutual understandings about the right to choose their own mates.

Dermot and Rowena had mated. Her pups would come soon. Already she had spent time out exploring, trying to find the perfect den to raise her young in.

"You are thoughtful, my husband." I turned my head to gaze at Tomura. She cleaned her paw and blinked her chocolate eyes.

"Much has changed," I told her.

"It has," she agreed.

"What would you think," I paused, needing her reaction so I would know if the others might agree, "Of finding a house to live in instead of the school?"

"Hmmm." She sat, her thin tail draped over her brown paws, the tip rising and falling.

"I like the idea." Starlite appeared beside us. "But what of Callie?"

"She would come with us. If she wants." I knew I would like our elder with us. She would be needed to tell tales to my new kittens.

My silver furred mate scrunched down, tucking her paws under her for warmth. "Callie may choose to stay here. She might not like traveling in the snow."

"She is older, Word Warrior." Lara joined us, sitting proudly beside me.

Mitzy bounded up. "What's going on?"

Tomura shared my thoughts.

The lovely Calico gazed at me with her yellow-brown eyes. "I've been thinking the same."

"Then perhaps," Tomura spoke as was her right as first female, "We should explore and find us a new den."

"There is one place," Lara ventured. "I have seen it on my hunting trips with my sons."

"Is it close?" Mizty asked.

"It isn't far. I think those who lived there before had felines. There are fine places to scratch and much soft fabric to lie on and build new nests with."

"Show us," I insisted.

We trotted out of the school warily as the dark was beginning. Lara led us to the place between the houses where the snow piled deep. She turned and turned again following a path she knew but we did not. Sitting on a slight rise was a house surprising intact and not crushed as those around it. Outside an old mailbox rusted, red rivets staining the snow as if it were dying prey.

My wife went to a ground level window and wiggled inside. We all did the same. Inside was a pale room, two broken chairs, and other objects I could not identify.

"There's a lower room and several upstairs. Plenty of space to raise our kittens."

So at least another of my wives had been thinking of a possible new den. Lara had already checked to see if the house would good a place.

"What odd things," Starlite observed. She jumped on a box that shifted. Gracefully she balanced herself so she would not fall.

I leaped onto another box to see what she had found. On a shelf sat a small house. The outside seemed be like the brick of the school and human figures and animals were inside. The top section had beds and other stuff, and I thought I saw a very small cat. The lower section had creatures I could now identify. Cows, horses, sheep, pigs, goats, even a dog. There were more cats as well.

"Why would a small house be inside a large one?" Starlite cocked her head puzzled.

"I've read humans had all sorts of hobbies." Lara informed Starlite. "I think one human here did what they called miniature dollhouses. If you look around," she sat down on the brown and stained carpet. "You'll see even more of them."

My mate was right. All around the room little houses of different sizes sat on shelves. They were different colors and seemed to have people and animals in them. I noticed there were a lot of cats.

"Strange thing for a human to do." Mitzy jumped up into a blue chair. "Might be a good place for naps."

"From what we've read, they did many strange things." I jumped to the floor. I wanted to see more of this house. Going down first, I found another room at the bottom of the stairs. It seemed warmer. Here too houses sat on shelves and very large ones on tables. Along a wall I found a small hole. It led to a tiny dark room and had smelly boxes in it. I quickly left.

Running up stairs, the next group of rooms had a big couch which had been marked by others of our kind. I think they were dead since no challenge to our presence was issued. Another held a table and counter, and objects I didn't know.

The last set of stairs had a small hallway. One door sat crooked and I saw even more small houses. One of rooms had a bed that would be a wonderful place to sleep and be warm. The last two had strange things in them which again, I did not know. Though the picture hanging lopsided showed a faded picture of the ocean with a net and seashells in it.

"I think we will like it here," Tomura said. She sat on the stairs waiting for me.

My other wives agreed. As did I. It would be good to den with just us and not share it with wolves or Spotted Ghosts, and all the other cats who now came to be taught.

Lara led us back to the school. On the way we talked about how soon we would move into the new den. Upon our return we learned many of the young females had gone into heat and with their chosen mates they had moved to new dens. Two of Tomura's daughters had decided to share one house. So had my foundlings Blythe and Ellen. Mitzy's had not nor had Sapphire, Starlite's daughter. Lara's three males had found mates with other kittens from the community, as had Tomura's. Neutron had no interest in females as of yet, nor did Clomper.

"Daddy," Nan approached me. "Jojo and I think we should go and watch the two leg burned thing."

She had asked me before and I had told her I would think about it.

Before I could reply, Tomura asked a question of her daughter. "Are you certain this is what you wish to do? Is there no young male here you would like to mate with?"

If Nan could have wrinkled her nose, as I had read humans did, I think she would have. "There are none, Mother. Jojo and I have other interests."

My Siamese wife glanced back at me. I knew someone needed to go and I felt my daughter would be safe with her wolf companion. "If more two-legs, humans come, return and tell me at once."

Her yellow eyes sparkled. "I'll tell Jojo and we'll leave at once!" She bounded out of the room calling for her friend.

"Well done, Word Warrior," Indrani complimented. "We need to watch for more two-legs. Perhaps Nan and Jojo will wait to establish their own den." Her long spotted tail swung side to side. "I do not know what the other young will do." I feared to know her answer. Were the Ghosts going to leave us as well?

She swung her huge head around to stare at me almost as if she'd heard my thoughts. "We will not leave you as most of the packs did. Yet, we have a desire for a den of our own. Cleo has told us of a place that stands high and has many rooms. The cats will not go there. I think it would make a good dwelling for us. When the dark comes again, we will go there."

I knew what she spoke of. A three story hotel, as the humans would have called it. It was not far from us. At least they would not abandon us as had two of the wolf packs.

"A good choice," I told her.

"We like the high places." She padded off no doubt to tell Jyotis and Valmiki.

"Do not worry, Word Warrior." Starlite stood beside me. "Not all will leave."

"You 'see' this?"

She didn't answer my question. "Mute will stay as will Sasha."

With Mute's fascination for the computer, I somehow thought her words were more observation than her 'sight'.

"So, husband," Lara prompted. "How soon do we wish to move to our new den?"

"I think we should go when the Spotted Ghosts do."

Mitzy spoke up. "Some of our kittens will be going with us."

"And mine," Lara added.

When dark fell again we gathered at the door of the school. Mixed were my feelings on the matter. The building had sheltered us through many storms, and I had memories of all the times we shared together. It had built a strong beginning.

Neutron and Sapphire refused to leave. "Our home is here, Father. We will stay."

Starlite touched both their noses. "We will not be far if you need us."

I watched as the Ghosts trotted down the hill. Their white fur shimmered in the moonlight. At least it had not stormed. Nan and Jojo approached us. They too, would leave now.

Lavena and Rowena came to bid Jojo farewell. The rest of their packs were off hunting. Iden had recovered, but he was still weak. He sat on the step near Rowena.

"We will return if the two-legs come," Nan said. "Don't worry about me, Daddy. Jojo will take care of me. So will The Provider."

The young wolf woofed as if to confirm what my daughter said. He rubbed against Rowena, and Lavena, and also Mitzy. My daughter touched my nose, and her mother's.

"Don't worry," Nan told us again.

Together the pair walked down the incline. They had far to go. I prayed to The Provider they would be kept safe. I hoped the two legs would not come searching.

Callie finally had deigned to join us. She hadn't decided what she wanted to do until we got ready to leave. "New kittens to teach, hmmm, better than telling my stories to those who are not my Starlite's."

We trotted up the hill away from the school. Rowena followed us part of the way before she returned. I wondered where she would birth her pups.

The light from the moon made it easy for us to find our way between the houses to our new den. We all went through the window and stopped briefly to rest and wash the wet snow from our paws.

"The big room upstairs will make a good place to sleep," Mitzy said.

The others agreed and we climbed two sets of stairs. The nearly grown kittens bounded ahead of us, exploring the rooms and playing a game of chase.

Callie groused, "Time to sleep, not play." Still, she did not try to stop their fun.

My wives went up to the bed. Callie chose to take the shredded piece of furniture while my young still played.

"I'll sleep here." She curled into a tight ball and closed her eyes.

My tail twitched and I didn't know why I was so uneasy. Perhaps it was the new den; perhaps it was the feeling of something coming. I did not know.

I only hoped The Provider would protect us.

~ * ~

Mute had noticed the cats leaving. He watched from the window as many disappeared into the various houses close to the school. Even Word Warrior and his females had left, as had most of his kittens. The only two who remained where those who had a strong interest in Science. They'd moved one of the nests into a closet.

Sasha indicated she wanted to leave the nest so he took her place to keep their kittens warm. He discovered two were male and one was female. Later, when they were old enough to leave alone, he would have his mate go with him to the computer and find out what she had chosen to name them.

When Sasha returned she brought a dead rat. They shared the kill, cleaned each other and she crawled back into the nest for a well deserved nap. The kittens snuggled close and took her tits to feed.

He watched them for a bit. They were so tiny. He would have to protect them so they could grow up and be strong. When they were older, he would teach them about the computer.

Speaking of it, he left his sleeping mate and again went to the library. Many books were still open on the carpet and he bypassed those to hop up on the counter. He was about to turn it on when it flashed and flashed again before going back to a totally black screen. Having no idea what had just happened, he turned it back on, and taught himself a new program he had read about.

When day came he turned it off and hunted. He took a large rat back to his mate. She still slept. When she woke she'd have food. He nibbled on part of it, washed his face, and curled into a tight ball next to his mate.

Chapter 22

At sunrise, Nan and Jojo took shelter in a strange building. The bottom was slender with what looked like a huge light at the very top. Nan had read about humans using lights to see during the dark. There were snow covered mounds in a huge open space surrounded by metal fencing. They'd found a huge hole in the jagged metal and the door to the structure was long gone. They both gazed up at the spiral stairs and climbed them, finally finding a dry place to sleep on the second level.

Jojo crawled under what Nan knew to be a desk and she snuggled against her friend. His furry side was warm and she slept until the dark came again. They roused and she stretched her limbs. A scuttling noise reached her ears and she stalked a tiny rodent. Too hungry to play with it, she crunched its neck and ate the entire thing.

The young wolf joined her. He found a few more and they had a good meal. They took the stairs down, even though she would have loved to have explored the building more. Continuing on they crossed some open spaces, saw more houses and some stores, until they could see where the crashed metal thing was.

Part of it was covered in snow and ice. The metal looked like a skeleton of a huge dead animal. Though what type, she didn't know. They went by it. It smelled of dead things and there was fox scent. She hoped The Provider kept the wily hunters away.

Together they entered the store Word Warrior had told them about. He had said there were warm cushions in the back, a place for water, and perhaps a steady food source. Her father hadn't been sure about that. The Snow Ghost, Valmiki, had done most of the hunting.

Nan found the cushions and her nose picked up the faint smell of her brothers. Jojo padded back up to the front. She followed curious.

She heard it then, the faint howl of wolves.

"Close?" she asked her friend.

"No," Jojo answered.

When they woke from their nap, a storm had set in again. Snow fell heavily and a wind crept in making their shelter colder. Nan shivered despite being curled next to Jojo. He lifted his head and whined.

"I find better place," he told her, rising and sniffing. He vanished through a black opening and reappeared quickly. "Come."

Reluctantly she left her soft bed and went with him. In the huge room were shelves and torn cloth. He nudged her with his nose. "Here."

In a corner behind some objects she didn't know, was a pile of cushions. She jumped up on them. Jojo joined her. They snuggled together and Nan listened as the wind shook and rattled the structure. She reminded herself her father and brothers had slept here in safety. Nan also had the protection of The Provider who promised to look after their well being.

When she finally began to fall asleep, she felt Jojo lick her face and sensed he would wake if she needed to be protected. As she fell into the dream place, she mused what it would be like if they became life mates, instead of just litter mates.

~ * ~

I stood on the window ledge watching the storm. Two huge trees laden with ice blocked part of my view. The drifts were so high I could have walked out the window onto them. Something flashed followed by a loud crash. I hissed and jumped down.

"Thunder snow," Callie commented. She continued to wash herself from her place on the torn couch.

My young were curled up on two brownish chairs and fallen asleep. Behind them was what I supposed to be a fireplace in the center of two wooden shelves. And in those, were rows and rows of books!

"A good find," Lara said. She rose on her hind legs and batted at one that looked like it might fall if she nudged it just right. It did and dust rose up. My wife sneezed several times.

"What is it?" I leaped down to join her on the plain brown carpet.

She read the title and I wondered what it was about. We pushed open the pages and sat reading. The wording was different from many of the books we'd found in the library. It did not recount history, or other such information. The book seemed to tell a story.

I sat back and stared at the pages. This was something new. Was this the human version of an Elder? Had they recorded their stories for future generations in books? Without one present to ask, I doubted I would discover the answer on my own.

"There are more books up here," Starlite called from the top of the stairs.

I hurried up them and she led me into a room with more shelves filled with books. They seemed different than the ones below, a lot more like I was familiar with and filled with information about the human world.

"Lara chose well," Starlite said.

I sat and gazed up at the walls. Not only were there books, but others things as well. Shelves with what looked like animals only different. I sensed they had never been alive. Pictures of oceans and fantastic creatures, more small houses, and dolls, I think they were called. There were other objects as well, including another computer. I would have to ask Mute how he turned his on and get him to teach me, so I could use this one.

"We should hunt." Mitzy stood at the door.

In my excitement over the discovery of books, I had temporarily forgotten my hunger. Tomura joined us and we went to the lowest level of the house. There we found rats and feasted well. Some tried to escape out the small door, but once inside, they were trapped. They were easy prey, despite the offensive smell.

Mitzy and Lara brought rats for their young and left the dead creatures on the carpet. When the kittens woke, they would be able to eat.

In one room above there were huge windows that started at the floor. My wives and I found warm cloth already there, and groomed each other before looking out. The snow blocked over half of it. My wives curled around me and I put my head on my paw. I wondered what other discoveries we would make about our new den.

~ * ~

Nan raised her head from where she'd been resting it against Jojo's side. She listened intently unsure of what she thought she'd heard. It sounded like thunder, but there was no storm and it was coming close very fast. Jojo turned his long nose toward her with an inquiring whine.

"Hear that?" she asked him.

"Yes. Hurts ears."

She had to agree. Nan got up and slowly crept to the front of the old store. The snow whirled up and she hid behind the low wall so she could see out. Jojo stood behind her. They'd been living there for one full moon and knew each and every hiding spot.

Outside something landed and she recognized it as a helicopter. Or at least, she assumed that was what it was. The color was different than in the pictures and the shape was different, more elongated like a goose. It had the rotating top and its metal legs sank into the snow.

As she watched several two legs jumped out. They had on bright orange colors, which made them easy to see as they ran to the metal skeleton. She couldn't understand the noises they made and it made her curious about how they communicated with each other.

"Nan."

She gazed up at Jojo. "What?"

"Look."

Shadows moved in the background. She knew the shapes. Wolves! "What are they doing?"

"Watching." The wolf shifted uneasily.

Two legs made a loud noise, pointing a limb—arm her mind identified and rushed back to the helicopter. From it they removed an object. Nan's heart beat faster. Knowing what little she did about the humans, she feared what they might do to the packs.

"Must warn," Jojo began to creep forward.

"Jojo," Nan twisted her head to look at him. "We have to watch only. My father must know what happens here."

He growled low.

"I know. But they chose to leave."

She returned her attention to what was going on. Lots of noise, loud popping sounds, howls from the pack. A pup dashed across the pristine and marred blackened white. A net hurled through the air, catching the cub and causing it to fall against the metal part of the machine. A high pain filled yip escaped, blood spattered, and the youngster stopped moving.

Jojo growled louder, poising himself to jump out of hiding.

"Jojo," Nan warned, afraid they'd be heard by the two legs.

A mournful howl rent the air, followed by every member of the packs. Even Jojo added his voice. The two legs looked wildly around seeming to just understand they had been surrounded. They backed slowly up and Nan suspected they were going to get back in their helicopter and leave.

"They're leaving," she said softly. She prayed to The Provider that was so!

"No," Jojo told her. "The dominant female won't allow it. They killed her pup."

Even as he spoke, Nan could see the pack hunting. They separated the two legs from each other and began a vicious attack leaving blood and flesh and torn fabric everywhere. The sounds of the dying humans rang in her ears like rat squeals.

As the sun slowly set the packs howled in victory and loped off. Nan couldn't help feeling just a little sorry for the two legs, yet she knew the packs had done what they thought right.

Jojo sneezed. "Much blood."

"I know." They had to leave. There were creatures it would attract and she didn't want to encounter them. "We must leave."

They went out a side entrance they had discovered. As a precaution Nan and Jojo took much longer to return. She didn't want to lead some hungry fox or any other potential predator back to her home and endanger every cat, wolf or Snow Ghost living there!

When the sun rose Nan and Jojo took refuge in another store. She stalked and killed a rabbit. Willingly she shared it with her friend. They slept curled together and left just after the dark fell. Luckily, no storm blew in to slow their progress.

Nan ran up the hill when she finally saw the school. They had traveled hard and fast and now the light touched the familiar brick building.

"Daddy!" she called. She ran down the hall to the room where he normally taught. He saw her in the door and left his class.

"Nan! Welcome!"

"The wolves," she told him what had happened. Jojo stood beside her. While she was talking Neutron and his sister joined them.

He slowly blinked. "Jojo, go get Lavena and Herne, and Rowena and Dermot. Neutron, go the hotel and get the Ghosts. Sapphire, bring my wives. We'll meet in the library."

Cats and wolf hurried to do what he'd asked.

Nan tried to relax, but sensed The Provider was about to change all their lives.

~ * ~

The news my daughter brought back was grave and a possible danger for us. I dismissed my class, as did my wives who were teaching and Algier. We all met in the library. Lavena and Herne soon came and Dermot as well. Sasha came and sat in the door listening. I assumed she would later tell Mute.

"Rowena is with the pups and cannot come now," Dermot told me.

I understood. She had young to care for. Soon Indrani and the two other Ghosts joined us. I had Nan once again explain what the packs had done and why.

Lavena growled. "If it had been my pup, I would have done the same."

Herne and Dermot agreed in low growls.

Valmiki spoke. "I understand as well." His sister growled an agreement.

Indrani licked her paw before she voiced her thoughts. "Two legs died before and more two legs came to see what had happened."

"But it took several full moons," Tomura put in.

The healer turned her large head to my wife. "They will come again to find their own. It is when they come and see how the packs killed them we will be in danger."

"If they find us." Dermot glanced uneasily out the window.

"Perhaps they do not have many of their flying machines." Herne sounded hopeful.

"Could be," Indrani agreed.

"But they have many of their other machines. We have heard the stories and seen them," Dermot reminded us all.

A deep fear chilled my bones. I asked myself if all we had accomplished here would come to an end. The two legs would not understand we were intelligent. They would kill us if they thought us a danger. Or worse yet, eat us as food.

"We must hide even better." Sasha walked closer to join us. "We cannot let the mistake of the packs destroy us."

I knew my daughter was right. We had to keep learning. Perhaps there was information in the old books that would help us defeat them, if we truly were in danger.

"And it happened far from here." Indrani flicked her long tail. "I do not think they will search far."

"And with the storms," Lara added. "Tracks will be covered. We will be hard to find."

"We were careful." Nan said proudly. She had learned well the lessons of hiding her trail.

"I know," I praised her.

"And if the two legs come?" Mitzy asked.

My eyes drifted to Starlite who had remained silent during our meeting. I wondered if she knew of our fate or if her 'sight' had failed her.

"What say you, Starlite?" I waited for her answer.

She shifted her fur glistening like the moon touched it. "Bast holds our fates in the paws of Mute."

I noticed the look between Nan and Jojo. I heard my daughter say very softly, "No. The Provider holds our future."

And I had to agree with her.

Postscript

Mute sat before the computer learning yet another new program. He had learned the human message boards and emails. The young male glanced down at Word Warrior and the others gathered for an important meeting. Sasha promised to later tell him what was going on. He just hoped it wouldn't affect his kittens.

With his paw he tapped a key and opened the email program.

He'd learned his computer ran on solar power and from Sasha, how it had made strange noises a couple of times. He had also seen the odd blank screen once, which had happened for no reason. He suspected that meant someone was trying to find out if it still worked. Or maybe they were searching for other survivors. He couldn't be sure.

There didn't seem to be any messages waiting but that was okay. He realized it might take a long, long time before anyone responded. Mute just hoped he remembered how to return so he could check for a response.

He'd thought long and hard about what he wanted to communicate and decided a simple message was best. The words appeared on the screen and he sat back proudly.

HELLO? IS ANYONE THERE?

Satisfied it was what he wanted to say, he hit Send. Now all he had to do was wait.

Other Books by WolfSinger Publications

Our 2010 Releases

All About Eve – edited by Carol Hightshoe
Eve - the first woman - some call her Pandora. Both the Christian and ancient Greek myths make her the reason man was plagued with the ills of the world. Whether in convincing Adam to taste of the fruit of the forbidden tree of knowledge or in giving in to her curiosity and opening a forbidden box that contained all of the plagues. Well, it's time she had a chance to tell her story...

A Cycle of Gods – Henry L. Lazarus
The Gods of Light have dominated the ancient world for centuries, interfering with human civilization. Now, someone is killing them. That frightens the Gods enough to send for the trickster, Odyl, the hero of the Minoan war, to discover the murderer.

With only his wits and his ability to throw fire to aid him, Odyl must somehow face Gods trying to stop him, make his way to Minos, cross the huge island to rescue his wife and solve the mystery of who is killing the Gods of Light and deal with a new god – a God of Shadows.

da sticks – Rich Kisielewski
da sticks, as seen through the eyes of Harry Mickey Shorts, ex-ballplayer turned street-smart private investigator, gives the reader a feel for what goes on in the corporate world of insurance plus a glimpse of life in the minor leagues, on and off the field. Elements of humor and tragedy, suspense and surprise twist and turn throughout. Together they keep the pace fast and provide Harry with a trip you will be glad you didn't miss.

The Hero of Twilight – Jason J Sergi

On a cold winter day on the outskirts of his village, young Bathmal's life changes forever. He encounters a knight from the north, who tells him there is more to the world than being a bastard, and even bastards can become knights.

Bathmal becomes obsessed with the idea and follows the knight from the village and commences on a life journey that will take him into the frozen mountains, across the sea to an ill-fated kingdom, and into the depths of The Black Realm of Hadez itself, there to face tests where success would grant Bathmal the chance to obtain everything he'd dreamed of, and failure meant endless death.

The Twelve – James K Burk

Valtierra, a city-state, is governed by archetypes. Every two years they choose twelve men and women to wear the masks and to become the Wise Old Man, the Fool, the Mother, the Harlot, the Warrior, and the rest of the council. But now Valtierra faces hunger, decay, and an enemy on their border and, when the need for leadership is greatest, one mask is worn by a foreigner and one mask hides a traitor.

Check them out at:
www.wolfsingerpubs.com

www.ingramcontent.com/pod-product-compliance
Lightning Source LLC
Chambersburg PA
CBHW060746180626
46818CB00002B/464